My Dinner With Michael Jackson
And Other Stories

by

Philip Graubart

This is a work of fiction. Any resemblance of any of the characters to persons living or dead is strictly coincidental.

FIRST EDITION

Copyright 1996, by Philip Graubart
Library of Congress Catalog Card No: 95-90924
ISBN: 1-56002-634-0

**UNIVERSITY EDITIONS, Inc.
59 Oak Lane, Spring Valley
Huntington, West Virginia 25704**

Cover by Judith Holman

Dedication

For Susan, Benjamin, and Ilan

Table of Contents

My Dinner With Michael Jackson	5
A Mystery	15
Death Takes an Assistant	28
Pro-Choice	35
Exile	42
Not In Heaven	53
The Day the Temple Burned Down	61
Converting the Jews	72
An Intermarriage	79
The Illness	89

Acknowledgments

Some of these stories have been previously published in *Response*, *Midstream*, *Beggar's Banquet*, and *Kerem*. Permission is gratefully acknowledged.

My Dinner With Michael Jackson

It all began one night after the board meeting. I returned to our apartment late, well after midnight. Michelle, naturally, was already asleep, as was the baby. I flicked on the light, removed my heavy wool coat, my scarf, kicked off my boots, leaving them all in a black lump in the foyer. I peeled off my tie, took off my bowler hat, quickly covering my head with a small knit yarmulka, and collapsed on the couch. My tsistis, my ritual fringes, popped out of my shirt, but I was too exhausted to tuck them back in. I was tired—physically and emotionally. The meeting had left me depressed. Some members of our synagogue school committee were pushing to "modernize" the curriculum. Add some current events, some contemporary ethics, maybe even some comparative religion. After all, they argued, we live in the late twentieth century. And our neighbors are all gentile. We have to adapt, they said, mix things up, modernize.

Some parents even pressed us to shorten our hours. We are overburdened, they claimed, our children are too busy. They have soccer practice, dance lessons, music classes, tennis, art, basketball, choir. Who has time for so much Judaica? There's more to life than Torah, they argued. We want our children to be well-rounded, they insisted, to have a variety of activities.

I argued back. What about commitment, I countered, our commitment to our ancestors? What about the spiritual life—the study of the words of the Holy One? What about tradition, our traditions which have endured for over three thousand years? How can anyone expect that this rich heritage can be taught in one hour a week? What about Hebrew, I asked—our language?

But I wasn't getting through. I'm just a poor old-fashioned Rabbi trying to serve the Jewish people and my community the best way I can. But it's a godless generation running synagogues these days. Yiddishkeit is in retreat.

I sighed, put my feet on the coffee table, grabbed the remote control and turned on the T.V. I quickly switched to my favorite station—virtually the only thing I ever watch—MTV. Then I shut off the sound (who can stand the music?) and watched a band of long-haired young gentlemen called Metallica act out a grim, morbid kind of fantasy involving graves, sick old men, insects, chains and dungeons. I closed my eyes and nearly fell asleep.

I was awakened by a cheerful image—the happy face of

Michael Jackson sitting at a dinner table drinking and laughing. I quickly turned on the sound. It turned out not to be a video at all. MTV was sponsoring a contest. All one had to do, was call a 900 number costing some seventy five cents. Your name would then be placed in a drawing which would be held the following month. The chosen contestant would win a dinner with Michael Jackson.

What the heck, I said to myself. It's only seventy five cents. And it's Michael Jackson, after all —a real celebrity. Why not give it a try. I picked up my portable phone and dialed. It must have been my lucky night. I won.

One month later, I am on a plane to Los Angeles—off to meet my dinner companion—Michael Jackson. Normally, I study the *Talmud* on any long journey—it gives me a sense of security. On this particular trip, I read a profile of Michael Jackson from *Rolling Stone* magazine. What a fascinating young man! He owns his own amusement parks, complete with rides, booths and all sorts of exotic animals. He invites, to this amusement part, certain children he has come to know—children who are sick, or poor, or simply so charming that Michael cannot ignore them. He appears to have had some difficulties with his appearance. There are rumors about him straightening his hair, bobbing his nose, even lightening his skin color. How interesting, I think.

We meet at a Kosher vegetarian restaurant on Pico Blvd. I am early. While I wait, I examine some of the stuffed dolls strewn throughout the restaurant. I recognize ET from a poster I once saw while studying at Yeshiva in Jerusalem. And there are other animals—bears, monkeys, lizards—all of different shapes and sizes. I pick up a large furry snake sitting on the counter next to my table, and feel it's delightfully soft texture. I am staring into it's eyes when he walks in.

He clears his throat. "Rabbi Loeb?" he says, softly with a voice so bell-like and sweet, he sounds like an angel. I look up at him. "I'm Michael Jackson."

We shake hands. His grip is soft, almost non-existent. He reminds me, with his handshake, of many Orthodox Jews I know. It's a handshake I appreciate; he doesn't try to tear my arm off. We sit down.

"I'm so pleased to meet you, Rabbi Loeb," he says softly, but intently, looking right into my eyes. I notice that his voice is high—it sounds very nearly like a woman's, and this pleases me. It makes him sound sincere. "I feel that we have so much in common," he says.

I look at him. He has dark brown hair which falls down to his shoulders. He has a face like a young woman's—really like a girl's. He is wearing a dark yellow, embroidered T-shirt, shiny purple pants with jewels at the cuffs and two white gloves. He has on some kind of eye make-up and blush. He is surrounded by gangster-looking body guards, dressed in black turtlenecks and coats, nervously eyeing the restaurant. I have on my dark blue suit, and I am wearing the blue and white knit Yarmulka my wife made for me on our second anniversary.

"How so?" I ask.

He takes off one of his gloves, and studies the menu. "I should think it would be obvious," he answers. "We are both part of oppressed peoples—nations buffeted by immense historical suffering. And we've endured—of course we've endured the sufferings—we've shown our strength, our capacity to cope creatively, and even to thrive. But the oppression has left its mark, wouldn't you say Rabbi? The scars are apparent—we've even internalized them—we reflect our hurt to the rest of the world."

"Well, uh," I say, taking a sip of water. Such an intelligent young man, I think. "I mean, we do what we can."

"Of course, of course we do what we can," he says, his soft, high voice gaining timber with the enthusiasm he displays for his argument. "And there, exactly—precisely—lies the problem. What we do is always a reaction to outside stimulus. And that can never, never be adequate—because it will never be enough for the oppressor. And it's not adequate for us, because we're not responding to our own needs."

The waiter appears. Michael waits for a moment, giving the menu a second look. Then, in his exquisitely polite voice, he orders a garden salad, without dressing. I order a humus sandwich, split-pea soup, an order of blintzes with sour cream, some pasta, french fries, and coffee. Amazing what one can get in a vegetarian restaurant. I am quite hungry; I haven't eaten since lunch. We sit quietly for a moment, looking at each other.

"Go on, please," I urge.

"Self-hatred!" he says firmly. "It's about self-hatred. We accept the critique of the oppressor. We grab hold of their disgust and turn it on ourselves. Jews are cheap—that old canard. If it's repeated enough, even the Jews begin to believe it. And they accuse themselves of this crime, and are embarrassed when another Jew even attempts to save some money. Self hatred. It's based on racial myths, on hatred, on prejudice. Like the idea that black symbolizes evil. Or that African noses and hair indicate an inferior intelligence. We internalize their absurd charges. We do! Look at me!"

I look at him. He does have light skin. His nose and hair do not appear to be at all African. It appears that the rumors I have been reading in *Rolling Stone* magazine are correct. He has changed his appearance.

The food arrives on a steaming platter. It is my food, of course, that is steaming—and plentiful. Michael is handed a bowl of lettuce decorated with one tomato. I look at it for a moment, shrug, take a fork, and begin to tackle my meal. At the last second, I stop. There is something I must say.

"My father had a long beard." I gesture with my hands, sketching, in the air, a long beard. "You know, like a Rabbi. And he had a dark coat, and a big, wide hat—one of those huge, real hats. He looked like a, uh . . ." I thought for a moment. "A real Jew." I say. Michael nods. "I, on the other hand," I say. I point to myself. "No beard, a modern suit." I shrug. "You see what I mean."

We both eat. Michael, lost in thought, picks at his salad and takes an occasional sip of water. I eat hungrily, the food is terrific. The rolls are outstanding.

In mid-bite, Michael puts down his fork. He shakes his finger, making a point.

"Assimilation!" he says with a winning firmness. "Assimilation," he repeats. "We blend into the popular culture." He looks into my eyes with a kind of pleading, like I'm the only one who could possibly help, could possibly understand. "But is it synthesis, acculturation, or pure accommodation? Are we bringing new and interesting things into our own culture, or are we just disappearing, becoming like them?"

I try to think of an answer. Who would have thought he'd be so interested in my thoughts? I am about to say something when he interrupts me.

"You know Rabbi, I've been to your synagogues."

I look up at him. I am genuinely surprised. I have never head this.

"Yes, yes," he says, "I know you're shocked. It was never public knowledge. But I was a synagogue regular. A schul goer! I used to attend services at Wilshire Boulevard Temple almost every week. I would sit in the back. No one noticed me."

"Hmm." I say.

"Rabbi," he says. "I'll be frank with you. It was a Christian service. You're fooling yourself if you think this syncretism—I mean the organ, the choir loft, the finely carved wooden pews, the musical arrangements—If you think that any of this is simply borrowing, or a creative mixture. You're not taking a bit of spice from the larger popular culture, the culture is swallowing you. What I witnessed at Wilshire Boulevard was indistinguishable from a mainline protestant church."

"Well, yes," I say. "But you see, not all schuls are like that. This is a reform . . ."

"Exactly!" he says, hitting the table for emphasis, and in the process knocking over his water glass. A few of the other customers look at us, wondering what all the commotion is about. Michael grabs a napkin and dabs at the water. A waiter rushes over and re-fills his glass. "Exactly," he says, softer. "Reform.

The very word. Why the need for reform? What is it that needs reforming? I'll tell you what. It's the concept of Judaism which doesn't meet the approval of the wider culture. You reform your Judaism to match their standards. And you rob yourselves —you destroy your heritage. And of course the ultimate irony is, they don't like you any better. In fact they despise you because, like the weaklings they suspect you of being, you give up so easily and with a disgusting sense of defeat you turn to them." He shakes his head in what seems to be genuine sorrow, and turns to his salad.

"Well, uh," I say. How does one answer such a passionate criticism? "It's not that simple, there are very good and loyal reform . . ."

"Oh don't get me wrong," he says, interrupting me again. "I'm not one to criticize. You see your reformers do exactly what I do, or used to do with my music. My albums are like Reform Judaism. They start out with an almost pure black aesthetic—gospel, blues, African rhythms—and then get washed in the worst white pop productions. I write the songs from an African base, but they are reformed in the records so the white masses can dance to them. My music is bleached, it's lobotomized, it's destroyed . . ."

"But it's good," I say. "Really! People love it." I sip from my water. "I like it," I say.

"It's garbage, Rabbi, it's crap. There's no heritage to it, no tradition—it's disposable. It sells millions, but it's ultimately worthless."

We eat. I feel bad, the young man is so clearly not happy with his work. But what can I do? I finish my blintzes and go on to the fried potatoes.

Michael sighs—a long sad sigh. "How I long to experience purity—righteousness—legitimacy. A clear and unadulterated idea. I'm so sick of the compromises, the meaningless mixtures. The synthesizers. I want so much to be part of something real. I suppose this longing was behind my flirtation with Louis Farakhan and the Muslims."

"Farakhan!" I say, indignantly. I look harshly at Michael. "But the man is an anti-Semite, a hater, a no good . . ."

"Of course he is, Rabbi, of course. Calm down. I was never won over, never converted. I know that hatred is not the answer, on the contrary—it's only through tolerance that we can ever hope to appreciate diversity. But you have to understand my feelings, my desperate desire for an African consciousness—or any kind of consciousness for that matter—that was unsullied by any outside influence."

"Yes," I say, "But Farakhan. The Jew hater . . ."

"I know, Rabbi, I know. And I knew it then! But you have to understand my desperation, the depths of my despair, my disgust with material and cultural compromise. I know he's a hater, a demagogue, a fanatic. But he represented, to me at least, national legitimacy. He was proud. He was an African American. And he wasn't afraid to articulate a black nationalist critique of white society. You have to admit, Rabbi," Michael says looking me straight in the eye, his non-gloved hand playing idly with one of his long hairs. "The black man has not exactly fared well in the white man's world. People like Farakhan don't come out of nowhere."

"Yes," I admit. "I suppose." He has a point after all, I think.

"But," he continues. "I gave up on the Nation of Islam. It wasn't the reality I needed. I'll be frank once again, Rabbi. They're fascists, it's time we admitted that to ourselves. And I have no interest in fascism."

"Good for you!" I say. I am quite sincere.

He looks at me. "Thank you," he says. "Anyway, there was still this gap in my life—this hole. Where could I find something true? Rabbi, I can't tell you how hard I looked. I tried drugs, of course, all of we entertainers have vast amounts of drugs at our disposal just ready for our eager experiments. I drank a little, sometimes no so little. I traveled. I spent time in Nigeria, Somalia, Uganda, Rwundi, Zimbabwe, The Sudan, South Africa, India, Egypt, China, Bangladesh, Tibet, Thailand, even Iraq. I examined non-Western political systems, religious institutions, folk customs, non-linear philosophies, languages. I drank it all in, Rabbi. I loved it, I'll admit that to you, I was fascinated, I learned more than I ever dreamed I could. But it didn't do. It wasn't what I was looking for. I returned an exhausted, burnt out spiritually drained husk. It was then I began consulting the Rebbe . . ."

"Excuse me?" I say.

"The Rebbe. Rabbi Schneerson," he answers. "The Lubavitcher Rebbe. The one in Crown Heights?" he offers. He thinks, perhaps, I have not heard of him.

"Yes," I say. "I am familiar. But you . . . ?"

"Oh, yes," he answers. "I've been a follower of the Rebbe for some time now." He stops now and finishes his salad. He motions the waiter for more water. Our waiter is apparently occupied at another table, so one of Michael's body guards finds a pitcher and fills Michael's glass. While he's at it, he fills mine.

"Excuse me," I say. "Mr. Jackson. You are a follower of Habad? I don't mean to question, it's just that I've never heard . . ."

"Oh, I've asked them to keep it a secret." Michael answers. "None of us needs the publicity, don't you agree Rabbi? With Black-Jewish relations so absolutely tense, so frayed, especially in Crown Heights, I just didn't think any more fuel should be added to the fire. And one can imagine the effect it would have on my career. There are enough rumors about my proclivities, enough cruel jokes. But to answer your question, Rabbi Loeb, Yes. Yes. Yes, I am a follower of Rabbi Schneerson, the Rebbe. I am a follower of Habad. I am a Lubavitcher Hasid."

A bright, serene, satisfied look appears on Michael's face as he returns to his salad. There are only a few leaves of lettuce remaining on the plate, but he relishes each bite, chewing long and carefully. I find all of this quite extraordinary. He finishes another slow bite and looks at me again.

"Legitimacy, Rabbi—it's what I was talking about. Something true, something real, something transcendentally meaningful. And I found it—at last—I did find it. I found it in the rhythmic swaying of the Hasids in the little schul on Crown St. I found it in their melodies—haunting, gripping, redeeming—the holy seductive sounds of the Ma'ariv prayers, the bold authoritative rhythms of the Torah service. I discovered genuine meaning in the frenetic movements of the Hasids as they pray—the aggressive dance, the bold, sensual, nearly erotic up and down, the sweat, the fervor. The spiritual heat. This is what I'd been looking for my whole life."

He speaks so intently he barely pauses for breath. I notice sweat beading up on his forehead, trickling down his nose. He stops for a moment to wipe his face and take a sip of water.

"And Shabbes, Rabbi Loeb," he continues. "I discovered the absolute joy—the cleansing, redemptive power of Shabbes. To rest, Rabbi—to really and truly rest—not like some lazy bum—not lounging around the house, and not losing oneself in a drugged up swoon, but resting by serving and praising the Almighty. Shabbes. Study, prayer, song, wine, fellowship, God, cholent, challah, an orgy of the soul, Rabbi," he says. "An absolute orgy."

I shrug. "Well, yes," I say. "I mean I like . . . that is Shabbes is important to me also. But . . ."

"Moshiach." He says suddenly, interrupting.

"Pardon?"

"The most important thing. Naturally. What really drew me to Habad. Moshiach. The Messiah. His coming. And soon. Any day now, Rabbi Loeb."

"Really?" I ask. "You think . . . ?"

"Oh, absolutely, absolutely. Without question. All of the signs are there, this is what the Rebbe teaches. The Gulf War, Rabbi. The ingathering of the Ethiopian and Russian exiles. The fall of Communism. This is Moshiach's time, Rabbi, I have no doubts whatsoever."

He goes back to his salad finally finishing it off. He takes a long sip of water. Our waiter reappears and asks if there is anything further he can do for us. Do we want desert? Coffee? We both politely refuse. A gentleman from MTV appears, and takes the check. The waiter walks away.

"You know that he is ill." Michael says.

"Who?" I ask. "The waiter?"

"No, no," Michael says. "The Rebbe. Rabbi Schneerson."

"Ah," I say. "Of course. And we all pray . . ."

"Naturally, naturally—we're all praying. Fasting, studying, doing what we can. I personally have added four special supplications to each service; I also study Mishnah an extra hour every day, all in the hope of convincing the Holy One to grant the saintly Rebbe a full and complete healing. It's the very least I can do. But this raises a dilemma. We are now faced with a problem. I'm sure you can imagine. You see it was always assumed that the Rebbe was the Messiah. He never came out and said it, there was never a dramatic revelation, no harbinger, no miracles, nothing like that. But still, this is what we all expected. The Rebbe was Moshiach, and, in time he would reveal himself. But now . . ." He shrugs, a strange look appears on his face. "He's quite ill. I've seen him. He can barely speak, he hardly eats anything. And he is an old man. It occurred to me the last time I visited him in his sickroom . . ."

"You," I say, taken aback by yet another startling claim. "You visited him recently?" I had heard that the only visitors the Rebbe was receiving was his wife.

"Yesterday," Michael says. "I try to fly in at least every other day. It's the least I can do, after all. Anyway, when I saw him yesterday in his sickbed—a pathetic figure actually—tubes coming out of his mouth, slobber dribbling on his sheet—looking all too mortal, all too human— a thought suddenly occurred to me. He is actually going to die. He is not going to recover, he is not going to lead us at all anymore, he is simply going to pass away. He is not the Messiah, it's not him.

"And then I realized something else. If it's not him, it must be another person. The Rebbe's teachings are infallible, his logic and spiritual acumen have absolute authenticity. Moshiach is coming. But it will simply not be Rabbi Schneerson. It will be someone else."

He stops for another sip of water. He is speaking now so quickly, with such fervid emotions, that he is becoming hoarse. He sounds oddly like an angel with a cold. Putting his glass down, he leans across the table toward me, and beckons me forward. I too lean, and we are nearly eyeball to eyeball. I can smell his breath—it is sweet and blameless, like a baby's. "If it's not him," he whispers to me. "It's someone else. Someone else now living is Moshiach. And I've discovered who. I know who it is."

"Who?" I whisper.

He answers by whispering back at me. I don't hear him at first, and I ask him to repeat himself. He leans in closer, and tells me his answer. "Me." is what he says in his clear normal speaking voice, his warm lips nearly caressing my ear. "Me," he says.

I lean back. "You!" I say, raising my voice, nearly shouting.

"Shhhh," he urges me. "Shhhh. I'm not ready yet. I'm telling you in confidence. Soon the world will know, but not yet. It's not yet time. But yes, it is me. Michael Jackson. Pop star. Spiritual seeker. From Indiana. I'm the Messiah. I'm Moshiach. I'm Moshiach."

I stare at him. He glares back for just a moment, and then motions to one of his guards. They flank him to the left and right as he stands up. I stand up also. He extends his hand.

"Rabbi," he says, taking my fingers lightly, like before. "It was a pleasure meeting you. And we had such an . . . enlightening chat—a discussion I will ponder on with great seriousness in the weeks to come. I'm so happy that you won the MTV contest and we're able to fly down to LA."

"The pleasure was mine, Mr. Jackson," I reply with great sincerity. "It was," I say—meaning it—"a real honor."

"Perhaps we'll meet again?" he asks.

"This is a possibility," I answer.

He walks out of the restaurant, accompanied by his burly companions.

I linger for a few moments, sipping water, leafing through the thick menu. What an assortment of wonderful dishes they serve at this restaurant, I think. Such variety. And it's a kosher place, and vegetarian!

I get up, and leave. I have at least half an hour left before I have to make my way to the airport. I decide to stroll through Beverly Hills. It is, after all a beautiful day. The sun is shining, the temperature is mild. I walk down Robertson Ave. admiring the fancy shops—the bright pastel colors, the luxurious merchandise. I see a lovely brown fur coat as part of a window display, and I laugh to myself as I consider what my wife would think if I brought her such a thing.

I stop for a second to listen to the sounds. Like in New York, traffic noises are everywhere. Sirens scream out, fire trucks roar down the street. Music is all around—it booms out of car stereos, blares from the boutiques. I notice, in the melange of sounds, one piece of noise sticks out. It is a song by Michael Jackson, and I am hearing it for the first time. "If you want to be my baby," I hear Michael singing. "It don't matter if you're black or white." What a nice song I think, what lovely sentiments. The music follows me as I turn on to Wilshire Blvd. I found myself moving to its beat, even dancing a little as I shuffle down the boulevard. What wonderful music, I think. How uplifting. The rhythm of the song moves me in a way I can hardly begin to describe. I feel wonderful. What a talented young man, that Michael Jackson. I can't wait until his next album.

A Mystery

Last week was the biggest snow we've had since we moved from Manhattan. My daughter Sarah had never seen so much snow. She was thrilled to discover that the drifts near our driveway were nearly twice her size. She brought a smile even to my wife, who claims to hate the snow, when she made a snow angel—not a horizontal one—the kind you make lying down—but a vertical one. She stood up against the area which used to feature our bushes, moved her arms up and down, and —presto—an angel of snow perched at the edge of the stairway leading to our front door—an angel to greet anyone industrious enough to visit us after the worst Vermont snow in twenty years.

Even Sarah stopped having fun though, when the snow started up again, blown by forty mile an hour winds, and the temperature dropped to 14 below zero. She became especially perturbed when we all heard on the radio that anyone venturing outdoors was literally risking their life. For some reason she deduced from that announcement that her mother and I may not let her go outside that day.

The fact is, we were all stuck inside for several days. We were prepared. We had lots of canned food. We kept the hot water running to keep the pipes from freezing. We had bought a battery powered generator, several flashlights and a gross of candles. We had bottled water, frozen meals and more boxes of cheerios than we would ever eat through two dozen snow storms. We would survive.

The trouble, surprisingly, became how to spend our time together. I say surprisingly because—theoretically—time together is what we'd been looking for. I have to work many evenings, Sarah has all the social demands of any popular seven year old, and Michelle—my wife—works all day at her law office. It was not unusual for two days to go by without my seeing Sarah at all, and catching up to Michelle only in bed. So I looked at the storm as almost a blessing; we could become a family again. And for awhile we did. But by the second day we could barely stand to be in the same room together. First of all, none of us could agree about what to watch on T.V. I was not going to sit through another Barney tape, Sarah would cry whenever I turned to the news, and Michelle just wanted the "damn thing" turned off. Also, playing games just didn't work out. I, frankly, am not a big fan of any game except Monopoly and Stratego. Michelle would be happy if she did nothing all day but play Scrabble, and Sarah just likes to throw things around, or put them in her mouth. In other words, we discovered this about ourselves as a family: time together was not what was missing from our lives.

Of course we also had our share of arguments, as the wind blew the snow into a rock hard drift against our front door, effectively locking us into the house. Whose turn was it to put Sarah to bed, to feed Sarah, to change Sarah's clothes? Sarah for her part, wouldn't dream of taking off her boots in the house, or wearing long underwear, or eating the peanut butter and jelly sandwich I'd just made, or stop throwing her milk on the floor. We fought about all of these things, and more. It was a tense couple of days, which is probably the only excuse Michelle had for blurting out what she did. "Why the hell," she said tightly, uncharacteristically using a bad word within Sarah's hearing range. "Did we move to this god-forsaken place anyway. Why didn't we just stay in Manhattan?"

Ah, Manhattan, I thought. Why *didn't* we just stay there? A good question. I chose to ignore it though, and instead helped Sarah peel the upholstery off the living room couch. I suppose I could have said, "You know damn well why we moved here," but the fact is, at that very moment, our precise reason for moving to rural Vermont happened to escape me. I couldn't remember exactly why. All I could think about was an incident that occurred to me around the time we finally decided to leave.

I was in my office at the Park Avenue Synagogue, half reading, half dozing. I was Assistant Rabbi at the time. I got a call from Barney Fierburg—a friend of mine who happened to run a swank East Side Funeral establishment—who asked me if I was interested in officiating at a funeral the next day. Marcello Rothstien, a Cuban Jew living in New York had passed away. Could I do the service? There was nothing unusual in his question; he often would throw funerals my way when there was no family Rabbi. I appreciated his referrals; I needed the money. He explained to me that this would be a fairly routine service. A middle-aged man had left behind two grown kids and a wife. It was a wealthy upper-east side family, typical for the neighborhood. No great attachment to religion, so a short service would probably be in order. There was only one thing that was slightly out of the ordinary. The deceased has been murdered. Someone had buried an axe in his back.

The Rothstien apartment was not unlike many houses of mourning I'd seen, working on Park Avenue. Everyone was quite well dressed. There was a gourmet spread laid out on the mahogany dining room table. The furniture was old and expensive. The people were sad, but reserved. The first family member I met was Ben, the older son, a tall, dark young man in his early twenties, who spoke softly with just a hint of an Hispanic accent. He greeted me warmly, brought me into the sitting room and introduced me to what he said was the immediate family—his brother Joseph and Aunt Ida, his father's sister. I wondered about a wife, but I didn't say anything. As was my custom, I took each of their hands, offered my condolences, and then asked them to tell me about the deceased.

There was a short silence as all three of them looked down at the rug, and gathered their thoughts. Finally Joseph, the younger brother, a short eighteen year old with light brown hair, spoke up.

"He was a saint," he said.

The older brother nodded, as Aunt Ida wiped away tears.

"He was generous," she said, her voice firm. "He gave money away like it was candy. To anyone. Anyone that asked."

"He was compassionate," Ben, the older brother said. "So compassionate. Those people that lived on the streets, the homeless?"

I nodded, indicating that I knew what "homeless" meant.

"They made him cry. He would cry his eyes out every time we took a walk. You never met a man so compassionate."

"His family meant everything to him," Joseph said.

His brother nodded enthusiastically. "Family always came first," he said. "Whenever we had a problem, if we needed advice, or direction, he was always there for us. He stayed up all night talking to me that time I was thinking of dropping out of Medical School. He talked me out of it, but he made it clear that whatever decision I made was the right one. He would love me and support me no matter what. Even if I ended up a bum."

The Aunt piped in. "Did you know that he prayed?" she said, looking at the sons, but talking to me. "He did. He prayed every single day. He didn't use a prayer book, he didn't speak Hebrew, but he prayed. He talked to God. That's why he was such a calm man, why he was so firm and satisfied and quiet. Because he prayed. It's not that he was religious, Rabbi, I don't want to mislead you. But he had this way about him, he was . . . well he was spiritual. He was a spiritual man."

Suddenly she started to cry. Her older nephew offered a handkerchief. She took it, blew her nose, but then started up again with a vengeance. Out of instinct, I reached over to comfort her. "That Bitch!" she yelled out, at almost the exact moment my hand reached her shoulder. I drew it back quickly. She blew her nose again, and yelled once more—in a firm, anguished voice—"That Bitch!"

"Aunt Ida!" Ben said. "We agreed that we wouldn't . . ."

"I can't help it, Ben. The Rabbi should know, he has a right to know . . ."

"No!" Joseph said. "This is not the time, we decided." Then the three of them took up a lengthy discussion in Spanish, obviously meant to exclude me. They did a good job, even though I'd taken three years of college Spanish. The only word I recognized was *muerte.*

"Rabbi Loeb," Ben said apologetically. "Forgive us. We didn't want to involve you in a family feud. My parents—my mother and father—well, things have not gone well the last couple of months."

"They separated?" I asked. Barney had told me that Rothstien was still married.

The brothers looked at each other, Aunt Ida stared into her handkerchief. "Yes," Ben said after a few moments. "They've separated."

I stayed for another hour, chatting pleasantly with the boys about their father, and preparing them for the service. Their Aunt said almost nothing the rest of the time, though she took a particular interest in the mourning rituals.

As I got up to leave, setting a meeting time the next day at the funeral home an hour before the service, Ida grabbed my arm and led me towards the door. The boys waved; I would see them tomorrow. Ida reached up and with two hands grabbed my head and pulled my ear towards her mouth. "She killed him!" she hissed, and I felt her hot breath shoot up towards my eardrum. "She killed him!" she whispered. "And he was a *saint!*"

Walking home towards Third Avenue, I noticed Rothstien's picture on the front page of *The Post.* "Millionaire Felled by Axe," the headline said—introducing the lead story. The two sub-headlines read: "Axed Behind Appt Building," and "Police Suspect Jealous Wife." Naturally, I bought the paper.

According to the article, Rothstien was no saint. There were shady real estate practices which had been under investigation for years. The writer quoted four or five "authoritative" sources who were pretty sure that Rothstien had close ties to the Mob. He'd been arrested four times for drunken driving, twice in Mexico where apparently it takes some doing to actually get arrested for driving under the influence. Then there were his mistresses. Five women in the past ten years had hit him with paternity suits. He was regularly seen around town with young model types. Until very recently, his wife—who had been a high school sweetheart—seemed to stand by him despite all the shenanigans. But his latest affair—with a twenty two year old blonde actress—had been serious enough to lead to a final breakdown of his twenty five year marriage. The article reported that Rothstien and his latest girlfriend were due to be married the next spring.

There was mention made of his temper. Ex-friends were

quoted who'd received threats and even minor knife wounds after petty, insignificant disputes. A friend and classmate of Joseph, who chose to remain anonymous, described the Park Avenue apartment as a "house of terror" where the slightest noise, or out of place comment, could lead to a beating.

Besides the wife, the article also discussed other possible suspects. Anyone with Mob connections obviously took some risk, so there was a chance that the crime was an organized hit. But, as the paper pointed out, Organized Crime doesn't usually use axes to get rid of people. The writer also mentioned a rather substantial trust fund that Rothstien had set up for his sons with the peculiar proviso of the boys having no access to the money until their fortieth birthday—that is unless their father should die before that. There was also a mention in the article of a sister—Ida—who had been quarreling regularly and heatedly with her brother Marcello over financial matters, and who stood to inherit quite a bit of money now that Rothstien was dead.

By the end of the article, my hands were shaking. There wasn't a person I'd met that day that wasn't a suspect in the axe murder of a drunken, philandering criminal.

The next day, right before the funeral, I met the chief suspect. According to the papers, no one was quite sure if Rothstien's ex-wife—the former Judith Rothstien—would show up for the service. She had every reason to stay away. Many of the mourners there would assume that she was the killer. Marcello's own sister seemed to be absolutely convinced of it. So even if she was innocent, her appearance in front of friends and loved ones would be—at best—awkward. And if she was guilty, coming to the funeral was downright perverse. Yet there she was; the first person—in fact—to greet me as I pushed my way through the heavy side doors covering the 83rd Street entrance to Fierburg's Funeral Home.

"Rabbi Lewis!" she called out, as I headed for the elevator. My name is Judah Loeb, so I didn't think to look up. But she grabbed me by the arm, just as the elevator doors were opening, and slipped in beside me. "Rabbi Lewis?" she said.

I explained to her that my name was Rabbi Loeb.

"That's not what the newspaper said."

"The newspaper?"

She took out a copy of that day's *Daily News* and opened to the second page. I saw a picture of myself hurrying out of the Rothstien's Park Avenue apartment building. I grabbed the paper, and read the short article describing, among other things, all of the various suspects in the murder. It noted the police's particular interest in "the scorned wife, Mrs. Judith Rothstien." The last paragraph mentioned that the "family Rabbi, Rabbi Joseph Lewis would be officiating at the funeral service at the prestigious Fierburg Funeral Home on the Upper East Side." I looked at the scorned wife. Though noticeably worn down—with small bags under her eyes, leaky eye make-up, and a collection of worry-creases across her forehead—she was still quite attractive. She was a tall brunette—statuesque and in perfect trim—high cheek bones with a shiny and absolutely perfect complexion. According to my calculations, she couldn't have been any younger than forty five, but she could easily have passed for someone in her early thirties.

"I recognized your picture," she told me, taking the newspaper away from me. "But I guess they got your name wrong."

The funeral home had a number of private offices for clergy. For a fancy building, the rooms were surprisingly cramped and poorly cared for. It was my practice to arrive early at funerals, sneak into one of the offices and go over my remarks. When our elevator reached the fifth floor, the floor of the Rothstien service, I rushed into one of the small offices. I was surprised to find that Mrs. Rothstien had followed me into the room. We stood next to each other, our bodies almost touching for a few moments until I made my way behind the desk and sat down. She also sat—on the one other small chair, really no bigger than a folding chair, across from me—threw her arms halfway across the desk, and laid her head down on her arms. It seemed to me that she was crying, though she wasn't making any noise.

I didn't know what to do. She seemed quite upset. That seemed to indicate that she wasn't the killer. On the other hand killing her husband could have upset her. It seemed proper that I should try to comfort her. But it didn't seem right to comfort someone whose grief was caused by their killing someone. So I sat there and did nothing. Finally she looked up. There were several tiny, ball-bearing sized tears rolling down her cheeks. I'd never seen tears so round. She brushed them away quickly, and looked at me. "Thank you." she said, exhaling slowly . . . "Thank you."

She must have seen how puzzled I looked—what on earth was she thanking me for? because she added, "For letting me cry on your desk."

"Your welcome," I said cautiously, careful not to give her the impression that she should go ahead and do it again.

"Rabbi Loeb," she said, suddenly looking thoughtful and a little frightened. "Do you think the dead live on. After they die?"

I waited for a moment, wondering why she was asking, and then started to mumble something about spiritual legacies and immortal memories before she interrupted me.

"No, no, I don't mean any of that. I don't mean symbolically. I mean really live. Can the dead communicate with the living?"

I didn't say anything.

"You see," she said. "I've talked to my husband. Since he died. Several times in fact."

"What does he say?"

She looked at me, perplexed, as if she was surprised to see that there was anyone in the room with her at all. Then she thought for a second. "Well, that doesn't matter. It doesn't matter what we talked about. It's rather personal, Rabbi. But I was just wanting to know—from you—does this happen often? Do the dead talk to people that are alive?"

I told her that I'd never known it to happen, though, of course, anything's possible.

That seemed to satisfy her. "Yes, well *that's* certainly true. That's certainly something I've discovered. *Anything* is possible. But tell me this. Aren't the dead supposed to get punished for all the . . . all the rotten things they did on earth. Isn't that what Judaism teaches us. Isn't there a punishment?"

I was about to answer, though I honestly can't remember what I was going to say. But before I could say anything, the office door swung open. It was Benjamin, Rothstien's older son, looking sad but strong and tall, even taller than he'd seemed the day before. He stared down at Judith.

"Mother," he said evenly.

She got up from the chair, stumbling a bit before finding her footing. It was then it occurred to me that she was probably stoned or drunk. She walked up slowly to Benjamin, put her hand on his arm. He stood still for a second, and then took her in an embrace.

The funeral itself was bizarre. The first thing I noticed, when I stepped up to the lectern, were four tall men in black ties, blue blazers, and sunglasses (the funeral was—of course—inside) standing at the back of the room. Police? FBI? Mob hit men? Bodyguards? Who could tell? I just knew that they didn't seem all that broken up by the loss. I also noticed that the entire third row was filled with casually dressed young men and woman—clearly reporters—scribbling on note pads, taking down every word I said. One used a laptop computer. Missing, as far as I could tell, was Rothstien's young fiance, at least she wasn't sitting up front with the rest of the mourners. Strangely, Mrs. Rothstien was right there—holding her youngest son's hand, sitting next to the aunt who was convinced that she was the killer.

In my eulogy, I talked about prayer, about spirituality, about fatherhood, and generosity. I said that it wasn't our place to judge this family or any family. I talked about forgiveness. The *Daily News* called my speaking style quiet and eloquent; *The Post* referred to my comments as moving and sincere.

The burial was like a scene out of *A Hard Day's Night*. As soon as I pronounced the service over, the reporters leapt out of their seats and ran to the Rothstien Limousine. Barney Fierburg ushered me and the immediately family into a secluded room. Luckily, he had set up a decoy limo which included live actors; the reporters who fell for it would be headed on a wild goose chase towards New Jersey. After a few minutes of awkward silence we snuck out a side door where the real car was parked. Unfortunately, there were a number of enterprising reporters who weren't fooled by the fake limo (apparently it's an old ruse) and they ran towards us. Luckily, Barney had another trick up his sleeve. He sent out a young pretty blond with sunglasses to walk towards yet another one of his limousines. According to Barney, she looked just like the late Rothstien's fiance. Most of the journalists ran after her, even more hustled towards her when she stopped for a moment looking like she was eager to talk. Meanwhile we made it to our car which peeled off towards The FDR Drive.

The cemetery was another madhouse. The reporters —apparently indefatigable—got through all of Barney's dirty tricks and somehow managed to beat us to the graveyard gate. Our driver, a big craggly faced old man who looked like he could easily have gotten a job with Rothstien's mob friends, bolted out of the car and started shaking his fist and swearing at the reporters. Meanwhile Barney called the police from his car phone; they arrived within minutes and were finally able to shew most of the pack away. It didn't stop all of us from being assaulted with cameras as we sat in the black limo. At the gravesite, I rushed through the final memorial prayers, my eyes still smarting from the flashing lights.

Towards the end of the ceremony each of the Rothstiens in succession—the boys, their aunt, and then their mother, took a shovel full of dirt and tossed it into the open grave. I grabbed a handful myself, threw it over the coffin, then led them all in the Mourner's Kaddish. None of them got through the Kaddish without breaking down and crying. Even the chief suspect wept her tiny ball-shaped tears. I sang the Memorial Prayer, and then led them back towards the cars. I was about to step into Barney's car—he would take me home separately from the Rothstiens —when I felt a hand on my arm. I turned around. It was Aunt Ida. She leaned into my ear.

"She killed him," she hissed in a voice I could have heard if I'd been standing 100 feet away. It was a hateful, poisonous voice, soft but full of power. I looked up and saw Mrs. Rothstien, still arm in arm with her youngest son, wince. There was no way she wouldn't have heard the accusation. Benjamin quickly ran up to me and apologized. Then he turned to his Aunt.

"Aunt Ida," he said. "This is not . . ."

"But she killed him," she said, right out loud, not even pretending now to whisper. "You know it." She looked at me again. "It's her, Rabbi. That bitch." She pointed at her sister-in-law, like a prosecutor, gesturing for a jury. "She killed my brother."

"That's enough," Ben said, and grabbed her, trying to wrestle her into the car.

"But he should know," she protested, struggling. "The Rabbi should know. Who else should know, if not the Rabbi?"

I stared at them as Ben finally managed to shove her into the black car. Right before her door slammed shut, I noticed her looking right at Judith, and Judith looking back. Both of them wore faces of utter fury—murderous faces which reflected a malignant hatred so electric that it could only be shared by the most intimate of companions.

The next day I made the newspapers. There was a picture of me jogging towards Barney's car on the *cover* of *The Daily News*. *The Post* also carried the story—which included numerous excerpts from my eulogy on their front page—though they saved my picture for page three. Strangely, both papers got my name wrong; they both referred to me as Rabbi *Robert* Loeb.

But the articles weren't only about me. The police were getting closer to solving the crime. And here was a surprise: according to an NYPD spokesman *all* of Marcello Rothstien's relatives—including his ex-wife Judith Rothstien—had been eliminated as suspects. This was the conclusion they reached after extensive interviews with everyone in the family. Apparently this wasn't a crime of passion at all. It was a professional (if bloody) hit. Creditors, disgruntled real estate partners, drug dealers, the Mob, who knew? It was a messy world Rothstien moved in. The cops were still working on it, but they were sure of one thing: it wasn't anyone in the Rothstien family.

Or was it? Aunt Ida certainly thought she knew who did it. But she wasn't the police, and I wasn't so sure. And, to tell you the truth, two weeks later I didn't really care. As far as I was concerned, the incident was over—I barely thought about it at all. It was certainly an interesting story to tell my family and colleagues, it was fun to be in the newspapers, I had a few laughs over dinner one night with Barney Fierburg. But I had my own life. My wife, in fact, was expecting a baby. I barely thought of the poor Rothstiens at all. Until I got the letters.

Exactly two weeks to the day after the funeral, I received a thick manilla envelope in the mail. It was sent to my office by Federal Express, with no return address. I opened it quickly because I was curious, and poured the contents out on my desk. It was letters—dozens of them, maybe fifty. I picked one up and saw that the addressee's name was blacked out. Someone didn't want me to know to whom the letter had been addressed. But the writer was clear, the signature at the bottom was wide and legible. It was the late Marcello Rothstien. Leafing through the pile, I discovered that all the letters were written by Rothstien, with the names of his correspondent scratched out. For the next four hours, I sat back in my leather chair and read the letters.

It's hard to know how to begin to describe the contents of these sad, sad texts. They were a portrait of marital hell, a picture of a marriage gone so wrong that one just couldn't imagine how this couple ever could have had enough good feeling to even hold hands, much less make love and raise two children. The letters were written to someone Marcello knew well, well enough to describe five years of intimate, humiliating mental anguish. Here is a part of one:

Last night I came home from the office. I could hear the screaming already as I went up the elevator. I stepped into the hallway—the apartment door was open. Judith was cowering in the corner by the kitchen, screaming at the top of her lungs. I saw that she was furious, and yelling at Benjamin. I couldn't tell what she was saying, she was hysterical. Clearly, she'd been drinking. She saw me come in the room and started screaming: "You Fucking Bastard!" over and over again. She must have yelled it ten times. There couldn't have been anyone in the building who didn't hear. Finally she jumped up and ran at me. She started beating on my chest. She was yelling, "You fucking bastard, this is what you've taught our children! You've taught them to swear at their mother. To say fuck you to their mother. And to hit their mother. You bastard. I should kill you! I'd love to kill you." She kept hitting me, punching me in the chest and in the stomach. When she tried to scratch my face, I had to put a stop to it. I grabbed her by the arms, and dragged her into one of the spare bedrooms. She screamed bloody murder, and even tried kicking me. But I'm stronger than her. I threw her in the room and shut the door. I told her to calm down. I looked back into the room, and I saw the kids staring at me. I felt my face and noticed blood coming down. It was enough, I thought, enough. I called the police . . .

He went on to describe, in those short, matter of fact sentences, how the police arrived, questioned everyone in the family, including the two boys. Judith had calmed down, and seemed in control of the situation. They decided to let the cops go without anyone pressing charges.

Another letter described this scene:

She came up to me. For once she wasn't drunk, or stoned.

24

Neither was I. I was reading the paper. I wanted to be alone. But she had to talk. She told me she didn't love me. She said she couldn't stand me. I wasn't surprised since I can't stand her either. But she told me she wanted a divorce. I said, fine—get a divorce—but I wasn't giving her a penny. Not a single penny. She smiled at me. She looked friendly, even tried to take my hand. Look, she told me, it's now working, we don't love each other, we're bad for each other. Let's just end it. Be reasonable. I told her I was being completely reasonable. If she didn't love me, she should just leave. But don't expect me to give her a penny. That's when she slapped me and called me a dirty son of a bitch. I hit her hard on the face, and she fell back. I got out of my chair and took a step towards her. She kicked me hard in the shins. I know she wasn't going for my shins. She was trying to kick my balls. But it hurt anyway. It would have hurt more if it were my balls, but it hurt anyway. I slapped her again, this time harder. I saw she was bleeding. She called me a dirty bastard again, and a son of a bitch. She said that all she needed was a gun and then she would kill me . . .

There was another letter that was equally horrifying, but quite confusing. Rothstien described a night when he came home late, apparently after being with a lover. Judith was waiting for him and complained about his odor—the fact that he smelled like a woman. It wasn't clear to me whether the person he was writing to was the lover, or someone else. I got the impression that he was trying to hide the fact—from the reader—that he was having an affair. But if that was the case, he didn't do a very good job, since even I figured it out after just two readings. In any case, as Rothstien described it, Judith used her favorite expletives (son of a bitch, bastard, fucker) and told him that he had destroyed not only her but the whole family. Their sons, she said, were both hopelessly messed up and insecure, and would never be able to enter into loving relationships. She also told him that both boys despised him, hated him deeply, not only for what he had done to them as a family, but also because he was a crook and an adulterer. That made Rothstien lose his temper completely—and, for what he claimed was the first time, he swung at his wife with a fist. Apparently he only grazed her, but because he was a strong man, even that inaccurate punch knocked her down and drew some blood. Judith, not really very hurt, popped up and punched Rothstien square in the stomach. For the next few minutes, like inflamed pugilists, they swung back and forth at each other, connecting just often enough to send them both to the hospital for stitches. For some strange reason, they rode back and forth to the hospital together in the same cab. On the way home, Judith assured her husband that one day she would kill him.

I left New York, with my wife and two month old baby, six months after receiving those strange letters. As far as I know (and I have been keeping up) Rothstien's murder was never solved, no one was tried or even arrested. It was a mystery.

Normally I like mysteries, when I was in college and graduate school I read almost one mystery a week. I was hardly ever fooled; I nearly always guessed who the murderer was—usually even how he would get caught. So it was odd that when I was confronted with this real life mystery, I didn't exactly care who the killer was. There were other, to me, bigger mysteries.

For instance, who sent me the letters? And why? Were they sent to the police also, or was it just me? And who was Rothstien writing to? It seemed like a lover, but would Rothstien really want to admit to his lover that he'd beat up his smallish wife? Lots of mysteries and not a lot of answers. I have my own suspect as to who sent the letters, and I *think* I know why. Aunt Ida was clearly interested in letting me know that she thought Judith was the killer. For some reason, it was important to her that I know, probably because I represented to her a kind of link to ultimate justice. And each sordid, bloody letter is powerful testimony to Judith's continuing, almost desperate desire to get rid of her husband. So Aunt Ida is probably the one. Still, I'm not so sure. That would almost have to mean that the letters were, in fact, written to her. How else would she have gotten them? But somehow those letters don't *read* like something you would send to your sister. I suppose she could have gotten them from some other close companion. But would a true intimate really give up such grotesque material about someone she loved? There are certain dark personal secrets, it seems to me, that we'd all just as soon keep hidden. These letters struck me as being so foul, so filled with banal but ugly hatred, that the first reaction of any sane correspondent would be hide them away, or even burn them. Yet here they were, in my desk drawer.

Yet the mystery of the letters was a sideshow to me—it wasn't the *big* puzzle. I couldn't fathom (and I still can't) the Rothstien Family. How did the boys really feel about their murdered crook of a father, their drug-addicted mother? Were the tears that I saw them shed for Rothstien at the funeral real, did they come from a genuine ache of the soul? Or were they a put on, show tears, the weeping of actors—actors so skillful that they perhaps even fooled themselves? And what about Judith, her odd-shaped ball-bearing tears? Was she crying out of relief, overjoyed that this cruel and hateful man was at last out of her life?

Or was it something else? Was she crying because she remembered a time—long ago and nearly hidden from memory by a continuing excretion of a veracious hostility—when she loved the man laying in the coffin in front of her. Did she recall that love, and maybe even feel it, if just a little and for just an instant. Was she crying because she loved Rothstien, the man she so wanted to see dead? That's the question. Can love and hate exist simultaneously—both directed at the same person?

Which brings up the last mystery. How does this happen to a couple? How does a family become so degraded, so full of decadent fury that murder becomes a real possibility? What combination of greed, vanity, lust, despair, passion, hunger, loneliness, contempt, longing and desolation produces this mess of a relationship? This is what puzzles me. After all, this was a couple that must have, at one point, had feelings for each other. They had sex; they parented children. In fact in my mind, I see them in better times, holding hands, walking as young lovers through Central Park. And I see more. I see them honeymooning on the beach in Puerto Rico, tasting the salt on each other's skin as they kiss and then make love on the sand. And more, I see them in a wood cabin up north, the fire place roaring with life. It is dinner time—twilight. On a whim, they bundle up and head outside to watch the snow fall in the growing moonlight. They throw themselves down to the ground, their fall broken by the soft snow, and move their arms and their legs—back and forth, up and down; they make angels in the snow.

Death Takes an Assistant

Rabbi Bibi b. Abaye, was frequently visited by the Angel of death. (Once) the latter said to his messenger. Go, bring me Miriam, the women's hairdresser! He went and brought him Miriam, the children's nurse. Said he to him: I told thee Miriam, the women's hairdresser. He answered: If so, I will take her back. Said he to him: Since thou hast brought her, let her be added. But how were you able to get her? She was holding a shovel in her hand and was heating and raking the oven. She took it and put it on her foot and burnt herself, thus her luck was impaired and I brought her. Said R. Bibi b. Abaye to him: Have ye permission to act thus? He answered him: Is it not written: 'There is that is swept away without judgment'?

—Talmud, Hagiga 4a

My study partner is an accountant named Joseph. He actually used to be a Rabbi, but found himself—in his words—"emotionally unequipped" for the job. I'm not sure what equipment a Rabbi needs, but I do know that Joseph is an emotional guy. He cries at the drop of a hat. Still, he's a learned man, and he has an elegant way with Jewish texts. We study together every Wednesday night, in his office.

At first we studied Mishna and Talmud. Then Joseph said he wanted something more religiously satisfying. He is a hard man to satisfy, religiously. I suggested something from the Kabbalah, but he snorted out his disapproval. "Impenetrable superstitious nonsense," he said. I didn't agree, but I don't like to argue. He suggested the Bible, which I suppose he considered religious enough. I was happy to go along. We've been studying Bible together now for nearly four years.

Tonight we're up to the thirteenth chapter of Proverbs (we're not exactly going in order). I read one verse, comment on it, then he reads the next, and gives his commentary. Sometimes we have long discussions, creative interpretations, long theological digressions—sometimes we just go on to the next verse. Now, I am reading. I recite verse 22: "A good man leaves an inheritance to his children's children, but the wealth of the sinner is laid up for the just." I shrug. It seems self explanatory to me, and not all that interesting. Good people do good things and get rewarded. Evil people do bad things and get punished. That seems to be the main idea of this particular book of the Bible. I'm not a big fan of Proverbs. I have no comment on this verse. Joseph reads next. "Much food is in the well tilled acre of the poor: but sometimes ruin comes from want of judgment." Joseph stares at the page, then looks up at me. He studies my eyes, and then looks down again and reads the verse to himself. And then he starts to cry.

That, in itself, doesn't surprise me. This is a sensitive guy. The Bible often makes him cry; *lots* of things make him cry. But I can't understand what it is about this particular verse that is so sad. I read it again, but I'm stumped. Meanwhile Joseph is still sobbing, and I begin to realize that this is not one of his ordinary crying spells. He's got his head in his hands, and he's rocking back and forth, moaning. I can see big tears leaking between his fingers. The page of his Bible is soaked. And he's not letting up. If anything, his weeping seems to be gathering force, like a river in a storm.

"Joseph," I say, quietly. "What are you . . . that is, why . . . ?" I'm not good at this. When Joseph's mother died two years ago, he was despondent for months. I could never think of anything to say that might cheer him up.

"Joseph," I say, louder this time. He keeps on crying, as if I'm not even in the room. "Joseph!" I practically shout. He looks up. "Why are you crying?" I ask.

As if in response, he blows his nose. Then he starts crying again. I lean across the table and make a motion to grab his hands, but he pulls away.

"It's alright," he says, keeping his eyes on the page. "It's just the verse. It means that people die unjustly. Before their time. And I thought of my mother and well . . ." His head falls back into his hands. He makes no sound. The storm has passed but he still hides his face.

I look at my page, and then back at Joseph. "But it doesn't mean that at all!" I say. "It means that ruined things happened . . ." I squint, studying the words. ". . . Well, it means that bad things happen because people make mistakes. People don't use proper *judgment*, so they get ruined. It's judgment, Joseph, not justice. This verse doesn't say anything about injustice." I look at the Bible again. "For that matter, it doesn't say anything about death!"

"No, no, no." Joseph insists, keeping his finger on the text. At least he's stopped crying, I think. "Look, Bibi, the Hebrew word *nispeh* comes from the same root as *sof*, meaning the end, or death. And *mishpat* usually means justice. Remember what Abraham says to God when they're arguing about Sodom? 'Will the judge of the earth not act with justice.' He uses the word *mishpat* for justice."

Joseph is good with the Bible. He has a great memory, hardly ever forgetting a verse. But he's wrong here. "Joseph," I say. "Look at the next verse. 'Spare the rod, spoil the child.' When does a child need a rod? When he makes a mistake. When he uses poor *judgment*. Look, the point of this whole boring book is that good people get rewarded. They *don't* die before they're time, that's the message!"

I can see that I'm getting nowhere with Joseph. He stares at his Bible, barely noticing me at all. It even looks like he may start crying again. Joseph has a problem, sometimes. He allows his own psychological state determine how he interprets a verse. His psychology captures his imagination, and his imagination captures the verse. Sometimes the process is thrilling, like after his daughter was born and he convinced me that the phrase "And you shall have rain in its due season," refers to childbirth. But sometimes it's a pain in the ass. And ever since his mother died of cancer, he's been obsessed with death. He sees hints of it all through the Bible. And it makes him cry. No matter how eloquently I argue, I can't convince him that he's just seeing ghosts.

I decide not to bother. "Why don't we just go on," I suggest.

He raises his head up slowly and looks at me. "Remember Judah?" he asks.

Ah, Joseph, I think. Not this again. Judah was a colleague of mine—a young lawyer—who studied with the two of us for a brief time. He died of AIDs right before Joseph's mother passed away. He contracted the HIV virus from contaminated blood, he was a hemophiliac. At his funeral, his wife made a scene by throwing his Tefillin at the officiating Rabbi. I wasn't sure what she meant by that gesture but Judah had filled me in. "She was showing everyone that he didn't deserve to die," he'd told me the night after the service. "He was a monogamous, loving husband who even put on Tefillin every day. It wasn't right that he should get AIDs."

"Yes," I say to Joseph. "I remember Judah. But I don't see . . ."

"He died before his time," he says. "It was unjust." He shakes his head, practically in disgust. "It happens all the time, Bibi. My mother—only 62. And you know how she suffered. And poor Judah, remember how he looked at the end? He was a skeleton; you could practically see through him. How could anyone ever forget his funeral? His two kids? And his parents crying?" He pauses for a moment to look at his book again. "Why does it have to be like that?" he asks. His eyes well up with tears.

I'm about to answer, but I realize that Joseph isn't really talking to me. He's staring straight ahead with a blank look. He wants an answer from the Universe, from God, not from me. And I can see that this is not a good night to study. Joseph's mind is elsewhere, in the world of the dead. I get up to leave.

"It's late Joseph," I say. I put on my coat, a navy-blue London Fog. He sits motionless, still staring. He's beginning to give me the creeps. "Next week, Joseph?" I ask.

"Huh?" he says, as if shaken out of a trance. "Oh, oh sure. Sure Bibi," he says. "Next week."

I step out into the street. It's foggy; the evening air is chilled—a typical San Francisco night. The old fashioned street lamps reflect through the mist like beacons at sea. I feel as if I'm walking on the ocean. I live several miles from Joseph's office. I usually take the bus, but tonight I decide to walk. After the choking atmosphere of Joseph's dark mood, I need the air. I head towards home, noticing that, though it's fairly early—not yet 11:00—the streets are deserted. And it's colder than I thought. I lift my collar over my neck and start walking.

I think about Joseph, about this evening. He really is obsessed with death, I think. I remember his mother's funeral, how he cried and cried until it seemed that every watery place in his heart would be completely drained. It occurs to me that his eyes have never recovered from that experience, that there is a permanent gloss of red covering his eyes like scar tissue. Since he lost someone he really loves, he can't stop thinking about death. I consider this for a moment and realize that most people are like that. Someone they know dies, and they can't get death off their brains.

Not me. I'm not obsessed with death, I'm not afraid of death; I hardly ever think about death. Because I know Death. Personally. I've seen Death operate. Death has appeared to me in dreams and visions, and sometimes even in my normal waking hours. I've had conversations with Death; I've interacted with Death. To me, Death is neither fearsome, nor awesome, but a rather ordinary creature with a job to do.

As I think these thoughts, I see Death coming out from under a street lamp. He is dressed normally, in his black robe, a curved dagger hanging from his belt—looking like some ghostly Sikh. He looks me straight in the eye, but pretends not to see me. For a moment I flinch: is he after me? But I see he is looking past me, towards the park. By the light of the street lamp, I notice that he is talking to someone—a short, stocky man wearing jeans and a black tee shirt. I'm surprised, since it was always my assumption that I was the only human who ever spoke with Death. But on closer inspection, I realize that this companion is also an Angel. Like Death, he has no feet; he gets around by floating from place to place. I move closer to them. I want to listen in on their conversation. I hear Death talking.

"I want you to bring me Mary Clarke," he says. His voice is high and soft, almost like a squeal, not at all how one would imagine the voice of Death. "It's her time," he continues. His

31

companion nods, and flies—feet first—off towards the trees.

At first I am astounded at the scene. Death has an assistant! Or maybe an apprentice? In all my experience with Death, I've only seen him working alone. Yet here he is, giving orders. I wonder how one becomes an associate of Death. But before I can give the matter too much thought, the assistant returns. He lands next to Death holding the arm of a frightened looking, dark-haired young woman.

"Mary Clark," the assistant says, with a slight wave of his hand, as if he was presenting her socially.

Death examines her carefully. He rubs her eyelids, runs his hands down her cheek, and pulls out a lock of hair. "Just as I thought," he says. "It's not her." He glares at his assistant. "You got the wrong person. This is Mary Clark. I asked for Mary Clarke. With an 'e' at the end of Clark." He shakes his head. "You screwed up."

The assistant looks strangely unconcerned. He studies Mary's face, more out of curiosity than alarm, and then shrugs. "So, I'll take her back," he says. "Be back in a minute."

"No, no," Death says, raising his voice for the first time. I look around to see if anyone else has heard, but I quickly realize how absurd that is. I am the only Human who can hear Death.

"As long as she's here, we'll keep her," he continues. "There's no sense in going back."

Mary screams a silent scream, like a pantomime, with no sound escaping her lips. Death ignores her. The assistant looks puzzled.

"But she has so many more years left until her time is up," the assistant says. "What do we do with the extra years?"

Now, for the first time, they both look straight at me. Their eyes glow in the dark, a fierce, shining red. My heart races, he's never looked at me like this before. He smiles, an ugly, mirthless smile. "We'll give them to him," he says.

Instinctively, I look behind me, but of course there's no one there. He's talking to me. I feel, despite the chill of the evening, a sudden warmth come over me. I turn my head back to the two spirits.

"This is a Torah scholar," Death continues, resuming his quiet, high-pitched tone. "This has become our custom," he says, turning to his assistant. "We give any extra years to those who study Torah." He turns to me. "Bibi," he calls out. "My friend. Would you like to add Mary Clark's remaining years to your own?"

I look at the poor woman. She is shivering with fright, her wide open green eyes a picture of panic. She looks at me beseechingly, but there's nothing I can do for her. Once Death makes up his mind, that's it.

Suddenly, I realize that I know her. She's a doctor at Mercy

Hospital, specializing in treating AIDs patients. I met her once when I went to visit Judah, the young Hemophiliac lawyer who died last year of complications from AIDs. I remember that Judah had raved about her. She was the only Doctor who didn't hesitate before touching him. Also, towards the end, when insurance money had ran out, she simply refused to take a fee. She even arranged for him to get free medicines. He was, I recall, especially impressed with her sense of humor, neither cloying nor morbid, it set the perfect tone for someone struggling with a deadly illness.

I also remember him telling me about Mary's family. She was a single parent—the mother of a ten year old daughter. Judah had said that sometimes the daughter would also visit him at the hospital. She would act like a nurse, he told me, offering him water, replacing his compresses.

And now Mary would die, leaving the daughter without parents. I—if I so chose—would add her years on to my own. I knew right away that I didn't deserve this. But did I want it?

"Will I need them?" I ask. "The years, I mean."

Death glowers at me. The assistant clucks his tongue disapprovingly. They know that I know that this is a question they're not allowed to answer. No one can know how many years we receive.

Still, I do some quick calculating. Mary appears to be no more than 35 years old—which also happens to be my age. Granted a normal life span, she could probably live another 45 years. Now, let's say that I live to be seventy five—a fairly modest hope since all of my grandparents lived well into their eighties. Another forty five years would allow me to live to be one hundred and twenty. I think for a moment. It's unlikely that Death—of all creatures—would want anyone to live that long. Which means that I'm probably fated to die before I reach seventy five—most likely well before. I pause to consider. How will it happen, I wonder. A car accident, like my uncle David? AIDS like Judah? Cancer, like my high school friend Sandra? Drowning? Burning? I had to admit that those were all possibilities—imminent possibilities. Unless, that is, I take Death up on his offer to add Mary's years to my own. I look at him and notice him smirking at me, as if he's reading my mind. He motions to his assistant, and they begin to turn away.

"Wait!" I call out. "Wait." I look at Mary. She stares at me, a bland expression on her face. "I'll take them," I whisper, knowing that he can hear me. "I'll take the years."

Death nods at me, then turns to his assistant, who writes something in a small red notebook. Then they turn away. I watch them walk into the park, leading Mary by the arm. The fog rolls over them, and for a moment they disappear from my view.

I run after them. My heart beat quickens as an embryonic

fear begins to form in my soul. I find them right away, but they're walking too fast for me. I can't catch up. "Wait!" I shout, and I can hear my voice echo into the park. "I need to ask you something!" They all turn, waiting.

"Are you allowed to do this?" I ask. "Just take someone's life before her time? You have permission . . . ?"

He gives me a pitying look, like a bullying teacher answering a rather dim student. "Of course," he says. "Don't you know the phrase from Proverbs: 'Ruin comes for want of judgment.' It means that people die before their time."

I am suddenly angry. "It doesn't mean that at all!" I say, nearly exploding with fury. "That's not even close to what that verse means. It means that bad things happen when children . . . I mean things get ruined because judgment, I mean justice . . ." I stop for a moment. I'm so mad that I can't think clearly.

"It doesn't matter," he says softly, and then smiles—a horrible treacherous smile showing dull yellow teeth in their final stages of decay. "It means whatever I want it to mean." His assistant nods. "Whatever I want," he repeats. They walk off into the trees.

I run again, but this time in the other direction, away from Mary, away from Death. Anger wells up inside me, joined suddenly—as my feet pound the sidewalk, and sweat pours down my face—with an overpowering feeling of fear. I run straight for three miles. As I reach my street—the sidewalk just below my apartment, my heart nearly bursting out of my chest, I am astonished to feel an uncontrollable urge to scream. I do, I scream—with all my might—though it's a sound that no one hears.

Pro-Choice

I am studying the menu at Paul and Elizabeth's—an upscale vegetarian restaurant in downtown Northhampton. As usual, I am pleased at how many items there are on the menu that I can actually order. I keep kosher, normally my choices at restaurants are limited to one or two dishes—maybe some fish or pasta. But Paul and Elizabeth's not only provides a great variety of interesting vegetarian options, it also offers fake meat items. If I so choose, I can—in good conscience—order sweet and sour pork, or spare ribs, or even veal parmigiana. The menu opens up to me a world of choices that I don't normally have.

Today, however, it's hard to concentrate on food. I just found out how ill my father really is. Doctor Levine met with my sister and me just a few hours ago and told us something that I guess I'd suspected for a while but hadn't really wanted to admit—that there really wasn't any hope. My father was going to die. According to the doctor, it was a matter of several months, maybe less. My sister is still in denial, she wants us to see another doctor, to go through another round of tests, to look around and see if there are any experimental treatments we haven't heard about. She cornered me in the small, drab waiting room outside the ICU and got me to agree to meet with a friend of her husband's—a more "progressive" naturalistic doctor. I went along, but at this point I know that I'm just humoring her. My father's going to die, soon. No decision we make can change that.

Naturally, I'm devastated. Our mother died just three years ago in a freak car accident. And my father is still a young man—not even sixty five. And I'm too young to be without parents; I feel that deep in my bones. I'll miss him terribly. But liver cancer is incurable—inexorable, deadly. There's nothing more we can do. I take a sip of water.

The waiter approaches me—a polite sad-faced young Korean whom I've gotten to know pretty well in my years eating at this restaurant—but I wave him off. I'm not ready yet, I've barely even looked at the menu. I start to really focus on my choices when I'm astonished to see two angels pull up chairs and join me at my table. I say "angels" because I'm not at all sure how else to describe them. They're certainly not human. They have translucent, almost transparent skin. They are dressed in flowing white robes. And protruding from their backs are a pair of large, ridged appendages that curve around the top of their heads and wind down toward their legs and then back into their ribs, and looks like—well wings. They look like my vision of angels as a child, with robes, wings, beatific smiling faces, everything but the halos.

The first thing I do, after dropping my menu on the floor, is look around to see if anyone else in the restaurant has notices these odd creatures. But no one seems at all perturbed. My waiter nonchalantly scoops up my menu, puts it back on the table without saying a word, and scurries off. A middle aged couple I know slightly walks into the restaurant; they smile and wave at me, but don't seem to notice anything peculiar. No one does. I'm about to bolt out of my seat when one of the angels speaks.

"You're the only one who sees us as angels," he says in an oddly androgynous but still clear, bell-like voice, that could as easily sound as natural coming from a young woman as a boy, or even a slightly effeminate man.

"Everyone else sees us as normally dressed adult males," says the other, with the same voice. And, as if in response, the waiter comes by with two more menus.

"We can read your mind," the first one says. "All angels can read minds," he informs me.

I am terrified. Why would angels be joining me for lunch, I think to myself. Am I dead?

"Of course not," says the second angel out loud. I realize that his voice is quite soothing. I feel myself beginning to relax. "And, by the way, we would never hurt you," he says. "We couldn't."

Just then the waiter comes by and asks if we're ready to order. Without hesitation, the two angels order a plate of mock spare ribs. Then they look at me with fierce concentration, as if my choice of food is of immense importance. I hesitate for a moment and order sweet and sour 'chicken.'

"Ah," says the first angel smiling with delight.

"Oh," says the other, nodding sagely, as if responding to an pronouncement of extreme profundity.

The waiter shrugs, and sets off to deliver our order.

I turn back to the angels. "We're her to watch you, Mr. Loeb," says the first one, who seems to be the spokesman. "We've taken an interest in you. You fascinate us, Mr. Loeb, in so many ways. Actually, would you mind if we called you Judah. We feel very close to you, even though we've just met. By the way, my name is Xlzcvhuhgkmnpknigst," he says. "This," he continues, gesturing toward his companion, "is Xlzcvhuhgkmnpknigsz."

"Hmm," I say.

"They are Akkadian names," he explains. I stare at him. I

36

can see the red and white lines of his seat cushion through his transparent chest.

"But I see this is a little much for you to take in right away," he continues, his voice reminding me of a religious song. "We'll leave you now. We know you have a lot to think about. But, if you don't mind, we'll be popping by often the next couple of weeks."

"We're really *quite* interested in you, Judah," the other one says.

The first one nods in agreement. "More than you could possibly know," he says, and they walk off. As they go through the restaurant door, I could swear I see them flap their wings and fly off. A moment later, the waiter shows up with three steaming plate-fulls. He looks around, confused.

"Never mind," I say. "Wrap it all up and I'll take it home. I'm not really hungry right now."

He shrugs. "It's your choice," he says.

They pop up again a few days later at the grocery store. I'm not quite as startled this time, in fact I'd had a feeling that they might show up. After the experience at Paul and Elizabeth's, it's occurred to me that perhaps they have a special interest in food. After all, angels don't eat, at least I assume they don't. And, as it happens, food is a particular interest of mine. They're interested in me, I think, because I'm a connoisseur of both food and eating. In fact, they catch me in the gourmet section of the store. I'm deciding which type of vegetarian broth to use for my lentil soup recipe. Erica, my latest girlfriend, is coming to dinner tonight. It's an important date. She's never been to my apartment before and we're on the verge of becoming serious. In fact, if it weren't for my father's illness—with my constant visits to the hospital and even more my melancholy preoccupation with his coming death—I'm sure that Erica and I would have progressed much farther than we have up to this point. But tonight I have no plans to visit the hospital. I'm looking forward to a quiet evening at home—just the two of us.

I take a moment to study the angels. I realize now how beautiful they really are; they are smiling wonderfully. They radiate a kind of glow of warmth and acceptance. I am no longer the least bit alarmed at their presence. On the contrary, I'm glad that—for whatever reason—they've chosen to spend time with me. I smile back.

"Please," the first one says. "Continue with what you were doing. Don't let us interrupt you."

"Yes, yes," says the other one, eagerly. "Please continue. We'll just observe."

Nodding at them, I reach for a can of tomato soup. As I toss the can into my grocery cart, the angels let out a sigh, a ringing, giggly noise which sounds like the cooing of well-fed, satisfied infants. I can't help but chuckle at their delight, though I have no idea what I'm doing that makes them so happy. I think for a moment, then head towards the produce section, the angels following right behind, their wings swaying slightly as they move. I must decide which vegetables I want for the salad. As I grab a head of Romaine lettuce, I hear a slight gasp from one of the angels which sounds almost like a cry of sexual pleasure. Surprised, I turn to stare at them, but they've already disappeared.

They show up again several hours later in my apartment, right as my phone rings. It's my sister. She has to leave the hospital, her daughter has the flu and she needs to spend some time at home. Can I come to the hospital for a few hours, just until Dad falls asleep?

I have a decision to make. I can go to the hospital and cancel my date with Erica. I decide right away to reject that option. Or, I can tell Dina the truth; that I really need to spend some time with Erica, that I just can't handle another night with my ailing father. Or, I can lie, and tell her that I'm exhausted, that I might be coming down with something, that it's probably unwise for me to visit Dad tonight and expose him to whatever bug I'm carrying. I look at the angels, at their identical faces. I remember that they can read my mind. Yet their look is so serenely empathetic, I'm not at all afraid of what they think of me. I sense instinctively that they're on my side, no matter what I choose to do. I tell my sister that I can't possibly make it to the hospital. I'm getting sick; I'm coming down with something. She tells me she understands. I look at the angels as I hang up; they are smiling even more radiantly than before. They are clearly overjoyed with my choice. They pop out of existence as Erica knocks on the door.

They show up two days later at my breakfast table. I'd been unable to decide on what I should have for breakfast, oatmeal or a bagel. The choice has me paralyzed; I've been sitting and staring at my refrigerator for the past half hour. Actually I'm quite distracted. Last night I heard from Dina that Dad took a turn for the worse the night I chose not to visit him. He slipped into a coma. I'm feeling dreadfully guilty. And if that weren't enough, suddenly things are not quite working out with Erica. I told her yesterday morning that I had chosen to be with her the night before rather than see my father. I expected her to be impressed with that choice, but instead she was appalled. She stormed out, and we haven't spoken since. I have to figure out what to do about her. Do I call her? Forget about her? Try to start up with Elaine, the new partner at my office? Meanwhile I can't decide between oatmeal or a bagel. I give my angels a wan

38

smile, and then turn back to the refrigerator.

Suddenly, something occurs to me. I feel like an idiot that I hadn't figured it out earlier.

"It's choices, isn't it," I say to the angels. "You're interested in my decisions. You pop in when I'm about to decide on something." I look at them.

They nod their white heads, looking slightly abashed. "Ye-es," the first one says, stretching out that one syllable so that it's practically a song. The other one nods again in agreement.

"And especially decisions about food," I say. "Like which soup or vegetable to buy or what to cook for breakfast. Because you can't eat, so you're fascinated about how humans decide on food. Isn't that it?"

They look at each other. "Well," says the first one, his eyebrows turned up in a sad, regretful pose. "Not exactly. Not exactly decisions about food. Not—uh—exactly."

"Actually . . . not at all," says the other one sadly. "It has nothing to do with food."

"No," the other one agrees. They shake their heads. It obviously hurts them to contradict me. But they have to tell the truth.

"Then," I say. "What . . . ?"

"It's just decisions," the first angel says. "We're fascinated with decisions."

I look at him puzzled. "Why?"

He seems to take a breath, though of course I hear no air being drawn into his body. "You see, Judah," he begins. "We are incapable of making decisions. We have no free will. We are automatons.

"We just follow orders," chimes in the other helpfully. "We're messengers." They nod in unison.

"I understand," I say. "Decision making is very interesting to you. You want to . . . study . . . to examine the phenomenon, to see how it works?"

They look at each other again, with the same morose, pale expressions. I've obviously gotten it wrong again; contradicting me saddens them.

"Judah," they say—in absolute unison, their spoken voices ringing as if in harmony. "Choices are *more* than interesting to us."

The first angel steps forward. It seems as if he's going to touch me, but he just bows his head slightly. "We worship decisions," he says with a hushed tone. "Choices are God to us. We think of creatures with the ability to choose as divine beings." He looks at me his eyes brimming with tears.

"But why me?" I ask. "Is there something extraordinarily noble or difficult about my decisions? Is it because I make choices so well, that I always choose wisely?"

"No!" they both say, quickly. "Not at all," they say.

"When we arrived here," the first one explains. "You were the first person we encountered who was pondering a choice. Our meeting you was completely random, an accident."

"I see," I say. I remember the scene at Paul and Elizabeth's. I was deciding which meal to order.

"Not that we don't enjoy your choices!" the other says.

" Oh, oh yes!" says the first one. "We've loved your choices. Every one."

"The fact is," the other one says, in a voice filled with reverence. "We worship your choices, Judah." They breathe quietly for a moment. "We worship *you*," they say, and disappear.

They re-appear several times during the next couple of weeks. They stop by my table at Paul and Elizabeth's one night while I'm having dinner with Elaine, right as we're about to order. I wonder, for a moment, what Elaine thinks of my knowing two angels, but I remember that she wouldn't see them as angels. I'm the only one who sees them as they actually are.

They materialize one night as I'm about to decide whether to watch the news or a rerun of "Star Trek: The Next Generation." They show up as I'm deciding to leave work early after a hard day. They come with me to the video store, to the florist, to the bakery. With each choice I make, they respond with either an impassioned, almost orgasmic sigh, or a soft chuckle, or a loud whoop of glee. At first I try to explain to them my rationale for each choice, but I quickly realize that they're not at all interested in the philosophy or even the mechanics of decision making. It's simply the act of choice which sends them into religious ecstasy. It doesn't even matter which choice it is. I can decide to lie to Elaine or be truthful, to visit my father or ignore him, to snap at my sister, or comfort her. It's all the same to them; they're all choices.

After a while, I just ignore them. I have enough to think about. My relationship with Elaine has gone nowhere, Erica hasn't spoken to me since that morning I told her I'd avoided my father to be with her. My sister and her family are upset with me because I think we should give up hope and just let my father go. There is no romance in my life, my family life is a shambles. And my father is about to die. Even if he comes out of his current coma—and it looks like that may happen—he can't last much longer. I'll be an orphan. I feel alone, already bereft.

Even the angels begin to cut down on their visits. At the height of our relationship, I would see them several times a day. They reduce this to once a day, then once a week, then once every two weeks. Then, their religious thirst clearly slaked, they stop coming. I make my decisions myself.

Three weeks later I get a call from the doctor. My father, who had actually regained consciousness and seemed to be doing better—had just suffered a mild stroke. He needs to meet with me and my sister, the doctor tells me. We need to make a decision.

At his grim, cold office in the hospital he tells us that with constant care—regular intravenous feeding and hydration, a stream of medicines—our father could last several weeks, maybe even a few months. His life would be painful, and he would—in all likelihood—not recognize anyone. His cognitive relationship with his children was over. If however, the doctor explains, we stop everything—food, water, medicine, attempts at resuscitation—our father would be dead in less than a week. The choice was ours, the doctor says.

It is clear to me what we need to do. Why prolong his (and our) suffering? Let him die, I think, without saying it out loud. My sister, however, needs to see my father before making any decision. We go to his hospital room. An I.V. line protrudes from his bony arm. His face is a ghostly white, nearly matching the color of his sheet. Never a big man, he's lost nearly fifty pounds in the last four months. His appearance is so frail it's hard for me to understand how what little flesh he has remaining stays on his body. It looks like he's about to melt away.

Together, my sister and I look at his face. His eyes are vacant; he stares past us, confused and perhaps frightened. It's absolutely clear that he recognizes neither of us; in fact he can recognize nothing. I understand completely that he's gone. I look at my sister. As she collapses into my arms, gasping, her eyes overflowing with tears, I sense with nearly telepathic precision that she feels the same way I do, that it's time to let him go. The decision is made.

As we stand, weeping, holding each other, I see—out of the corner of my eye—my two angels come into the room. My sister notices them also, though she doesn't seem at all alarmed or even surprised. I realize that they must appear to her as doctors or orderlies. We watch, as they go to my father and slowly, with great care, begin to disconnect his I.V. line. I hear them mumbling something to themselves. Staring deeply into their whitened faces, I am startled to see expressions of profound awe and reverence shine from their eyes as they go about their work, as if they were experiencing utter transcendence, as if they were performing a religious rite filled with holiness and the love of God.

Exile

I first met Mike in the musty attic of my new synagogue. I was trying to track down the cemetery scandal one morning after minyan, and I spotted him lying in a moldy wardrobe box underneath the large triangular window.

"Shalom Aleichem," he said to me, rolling over into a sitting up position. He was wearing a black stained white tee-shirt, and baggy gray pants. There was a large paper bag next to his box with what looked like an assortment of cans and bottles.

"Aleichem Shalom," I said cautiously, looking into his partially bearded face. I was trying to figure out how dangerous he could be. Was there a baseball bat around, or an old lamp?

"You must be the new Rov," he said, slowly standing up. He was tall—6'5", or more, and big, but he smiled and seemed harmless. "It's a great privilege to meet you. Usually I'm gone by now, on my merry way, but I have overslept. Davening is over?" he asked, and stretched his sooty arms. He yawned loudly, and smiled at me.

"Yes," I said. "Davening is over. We didn't get a minyan today so . . ." I paused, wondering what exactly to do. "I'm Rabbi Loeb," I said. "You . . . you, uh, live here?" I asked.

"An honor to meet you, Rabbi, really an honor—a great privilege." he said. "I'm Mike." He straightened out completely and stuck out a dirty palm. We shook hands slowly, and he nearly crushed my somewhat shaking hand. "Really," he said. "I'm sorry to shock you—you look all fermisht, but don't worry. Like I said, usually I'm gone by now. I guess I was up a little late." He looked around and squinted at the light coming through the window. "Sunny out," he said. "*Abie Gezunt*, thank God, so I'll be on my way." He started to lumber past me.

"Wait," I said. "Where do you live? I mean—do you live here?"

"Of course," he said. "I've lived here for twenty years."

"Where," I asked. "In the attic? Here?"

"Of course," he said. "Right here. In the schull, in the attic. For twenty years, abie gezunt. I watch over the schull—I'm the protector," he said. "I protect our Beis Medrash from the goyim. For twenty years. But let me get out of your hair—you've got your work to do. Have a good day Rabbi," he said and ambled toward the exit. "Just ask anyone about me, they'll tell you. I'm the shomer," he said. "Ask anyone."

I did, but no one knew anything about him. The custodian had been with the synagogue for twelve years. "No, Rabbi, never been anyone up there that I know about, at least since I been here. Course, I don't go up in that attic all that often—kind of spooky up there—but I guess I would have seen him at least one time. He said he been there for twenty years?"

I nodded.

"Uh-uh, Rabbi. Can't be. I never seen him. Should I call the police?"

"Not yet," I said.

I phoned the synagogue president, who was on vacation in Connecticut. It was summer, and I woke him up.

"He says he's the what?"

"The shomer," I said. "The guardian. Well, he says he protects the synagogue."

"From who?"

"From the goyim," I said. "I mean that's what he told me."

"Jesus, Rabbi, sounds like a lunatic. I think you're lucky you didn't get hurt. Are you alright?"

"Yes, yes, I'm fine." I said. "He didn't hurt me. I just—you don't know anything about him? He said people knew him."

"Hell, no, Rabbi—I don't know anything about him. I've been a member for thirteen years. "Look," he said. "He's homeless, he's Jewish. The attic is cool in the summer so he sleeps there. And he's probably a little nuts. This guardian thing bothers me. Call the police, Rabbi—do yourself a favor. You know there are shelters for the homeless in the city—he shouldn't be sleeping in a box. Call the cops," he said. "You want me to?"

"No, no," I said. "That's not necessary."

"I could come in," he said. "Maybe I should deal with this. I am the president."

"No," I said. "I just wanted to let you know about it. I'll take care of it. It's no problem."

"Call the police, Rabbi. It's the proper thing to do. You don't want him living in the schull. Get him into a shelter. Call the police. O.K. Rabbi?"

"Of course," I said.

But I wasn't ready to call the police yet. You see, in Rabbinical school I was taught to have great compassion for the homeless. I was a student (figuratively, of course—he was dead) of Abraham Joshua Heschel who felt that the quest for social justice was the highest form of Jewish religiosity. I worked at homeless shelters, served food at soup kitchens, wrote the mayor devastating letters on the plight of the homeless—my first real act as a Rabbi couldn't be kicking a homeless man into the street, especially with the help of the police. I needed to think things over—to figure out what to do.

Usually I studied Talmud in the mornings, after my trips to the attic. This morning, I had been interrupted. I decided to study a little in my office before coming to any decision.

I unlocked my office door and flicked on the light. I found Mike waiting for me, sitting on one of the red folding chairs I had set up across from my desk. He was looking at some of the papers on the desk, his curiosity obviously engaged. He looked up at me with his soiled, but gentle face, and smiled.

"Boker Tov, Rebbe," he said. "I decided to let myself in."

"Um, Boker Tov," I said, and walked slowly around him to my desk. I sat down. We looked at each other. "Uh, how did you get in here?" I asked.

"Ha," he said. "It was nothing, don't worry about it. It was gornisht—I just came in. Don't worry about how. Listen," he said, looking right at me. "You study gemmorah in the mornings?" I nodded. "Great," he said. "I used to study a blot gemmorah. I thought I'd join you. You need a chevrusah don't you? Everyone needs someone to learn with. Why don't I learn with you? What are you studying?"

"Gittin," I said. Would he know what that meant?

"Gittin?" he said. "What daf?"

"55B."

"Oy," he said. "Oy. The destruction of the Beis Hamikdosh. Being punished for our sins. Golus. Causeless Hatred. Exile. Oy. Tisha B'ov stuff," he moaned. "Destruction of the people—being forced out of their homes, murdered for being Jewish—that's what you're learning?"

"Well," I said, "that's what I'm up to. I mean I didn't start with it."

"Can I learn with you Rov?" he asked pleadingly, his hand stroking his five day growth of beard. "I need sustenance. I need the pure water of the Torah. Let me glean at your feet. Let me catch your pearls of wisdom, your sweet pearls. For the sake of God, Rebbe. Study with me."

"Please don't call me Rebbe."

"Gittin, Rabbi. The destruction. Guilt and punishment. Let us study."

Why not? He was harmless, and it would give us something to do together. I didn't want to kick him out just then—where would he go? I minded, a little, the slightly boozy smell that came from his breath, but I decided that I could live with it. Studying was a good way for me to relax, it helped me think. And actually one is supposed to study with a partner. I took out two Gemmarahs, and gave one to Mike. He opened it hungrily, and turned immediately to the right page.

"Rabbi Joshua," he read, in Hebrew. "Has said. Through a

locust and a son of a locust was Jerusalem destroyed."

"Yes," I said. "Yes. And through a cock and a hen was Tur Malka destroyed." We studied together.

After almost an hour, I asked him how, exactly, he guarded the synagogue.

"Oh, well," he said. "I don't exactly physically guard the place. It's just that I prevent harm from befalling our grounds here—our sacred grounds. My presence insures safety. My person is an insurer against calamity for our people—the Yidden."

"Like a good luck charm." I offered.

"Exactly," he said, shaking his head up and down, and smiling. "Like a good luck charm. Nothing more. Hasn't been a disaster here in twenty years. Since I started sleeping here. I'm the good luck charm. I bring Mazel."

"Mazel." I repeated.

He started to get up. "By the way, Rov," he said. "Why are you hanging out in the attic early in the mornings anyway? Is that really a place for a man of your position? It's mighty dusty up there, and cold. Not that I mind, but do you really need to be up there?"

"Unfortunately, I do."

"Forsh nicht?" he asked.

I sighed. "It's a long story."

"Ah," he said. "Ah. A long story. And I won't trouble you to tell it. I've troubled you enough." He walked toward the door. "Thank you for the learning, my Rabbi. It does me good. Shalom," he said, and walked out.

"Shalom," I said.

Why was I up in the attic every morning, traipsing through the moldy boxes, wheezing and sneezing until I could barely stand it? Because that was where all of the synagogue's files were stored, papers and records and ledgers and correspondence from the last ninety years. The synagogue itself was nearly one hundred years old, and all of its paperwork had been tossed into boxes, in no particular order, and thrown into the attic. Some of the material, though certainly not most of it, was quite interesting, but I'm not a historian, and normally I just would have let the papers be, as they had been for literally generations. But the synagogue was in the middle of a crisis, and I needed to wade through the suffocating pile of documents.

Thirty five years before, this synagogue—at the time a flourishing congregation—bought a cemetery and began selling plots. They held an elaborate publicity campaign designed to get our Jews to "be together at that final resting place." Brochures were printed up, a staff was put together, and many, many plots were sold. The Rabbi at the time, Rabbi Martin Siegel, apparently a dynamic and charismatic man, administered the whole operation, selling the plots, and collecting the money. The problem was, he turned out to be a crook, and a good one. Most of the plots he sold—hundreds—were nonexistent. The graveyard itself was tiny with barely room for thirty five corpses. Somehow Rabbi Siegel had conspired with a man who owned some land next to the cemetery to trick people into thinking they had bought eternal resting places. He made his money, resigned as Rabbi, and disappeared. That was thirty five years ago. Fifteen years ago people started dying. At first there were just a few, so the synagogue was able to make arrangements to bury people elsewhere. They avoided a tremendous scandal. But more recently, more people were dying—and the whole sordid affair blew up. The congregation split, then split again, leaving it with barely a hundred and twenty members. They managed to notify most of the buyers, and the remaining members tried to put the synagogue back together again. Of course, I didn't know any of this until after I was hired. Now it seems like I was the only Jew in America not to have heard of this scandal, but then I just thought that this was a formerly high-powered schull fallen on hard times. The interview committee, of course, didn't mention the phony cemetery at all.

Now more people were dying without their families having any place to bury them. One time—this was my first funeral—we even showed up at the cemetery thinking there would be a spot for the body to be buried. That spot, of course, had been occupied for many years. The dead man's wife dropped the flowers she was carrying, fainted and ended up in the hospital. That family ended up suing the synagogue, and I was named in the suit. We had lawyers who were synagogue members, but many of them resigned and just dropped the case. I was afraid not only of losing all of my money (not that I had any) but of completely ruining my reputation. So every morning, I helped my remaining lawyer and tried to find the cemetery records left by the industrious Rabbi Levine.

So, actually, the appearance of Mike the homeless man who lived in our attic was not an unpleasant diversion. It gave me something else to think about besides people dying with nowhere to go. And now that I thought of it, I began to feel that finding Mike could also be a good diversion for the congregation. For some time, especially before the graveyard mess, I'd wanted to start a committee for the homeless. These kind of social conscious committees were becoming common in the city, and I thought one could help revitalize our dying congregation by giving us a philanthropic focus. Mike's sudden appearance became my excuse for getting on with forming this committee. I called a meeting, in my office, of people I thought would be interested.

"Wonderful idea, Rabbi," one woman said, a pretty young

brunette with a flowered dress. "I've just been waiting for someone to suggest it. It's time we stopped feeling sorry for ourselves and started doing something for others."

"Yes, yes," others agreed. "A fine idea—really marvelous."

And so the committee began. We decided to have fund raisers, help homeless people get apartments, think about opening a shelter, provide lunch-time meals, and finally, to get the synagogue board to agree to let Mike continue living in the attic. I was happy.

On my way home from the meeting—I lived right across the street—I saw Mike standing in front of my apartment building, leaning against the entrance. It was a hot and humid evening, but it seemed that more than the normal amount of perspiration was streaming down Mike's forehead. He had on the same gray wool pants, and a wool jacket.

"Top of the evening to you Rov Loeb," he said, nodding gallantly. I nodded back and smiled. "Up for an evening stroll?" he asked. "I have things to discuss with you, weighty matters which require your attention."

"Uh sure," I said, just a little nervous, and off we went. I made sure we stayed on crowded and well lit streets.

"Rabbi," he asked, his large pale face screwed up in a look of intense concentration, "I have a religious question, a question that only a man of your learning could answer."

I nodded.

"When the dead pass on," he said, "and have nowhere to go—no final resting home, what becomes of the eternal soul?"

I stopped walking and looked up at him.

"Does the soul still ascend?" he went on. "Or is it too trapped, imprisoned in a nether world—neither alive nor immortal, at one with neither God nor man? Is not the soul—the essence of immortality—then in Exile, alienated from its homeland with no paradise to enter. Could we not compare it then, to the Jewish people—abandoned by God, our Temple burned and destroyed, our religion a thing to be mocked? Could we not make that comparison?"

"What are you talking about?" I asked.

"I have information for you, Rov, hard information," he said facing me. "The lawsuit which has plagued you has been dropped. Your ass is saved. But the dead," he said. "Where will the dead go?"

I looked at him. His face was twisted, filled with concern. "To another cemetery." I said. "It's really no big deal." We stared at each other.

"Yes, of course," he said. "No big deal. No big deal." He paused briefly and stuck his large hands into his pockets. "Goodnight Rabbi," he said, his voice suddenly compassionate, the haunting concern gone from his eyes. "It's time for the homeless to rest. Goodnight," he said again, and lumbered off.

"Goodnight Mike," I answered, but he was already gone. I went home. The next day my lawyer called me and told me that the suit against me and the synagogue had been dropped.

Probably Mike had overheard when my lawyer left a message for me at my office. I was unwilling, at least then, to consider him a prophet. In fact it was beginning to dawn on me that he might be genuinely unstable. He didn't seem dangerous, but one never knew with crazies. He was starting to give me the creeps. He came to my office every morning to study. He was, believe it or not, quite a bright student, his reading and interpretation were almost always nearly flawless. Unfortunately we were stuck studying the legends surrounding the destruction of the Temple, and Mike seemed to have an unhealthy fixation on that subject. And he wouldn't hear of trying anything else. "Exile, Exile, Exile," he once said to me, moaning, and pulling at his growth of beard. "To be torn from God, ripped from the bosom of the divine presence. A fate worse than being pierced with flaming arrows, worse than having one's skin flayed with hot combs, a torture reserved for the very hottest sections of Hell."

"Maybe we should try to get Mike an apartment," I suggested one night to the homeless committee.

"But Rabbi," someone said. "I thought you said he was happy living in the synagogue. We've given him a bed and a dresser." Others on the committee were equally puzzled.

"A man shouldn't have to live in an attic," I explained. "What will happen in the winter? There's no heat, no hot water. It's not sanitary. Let's put him on our list," I said. "We owe it to Mike to find him a decent place."

"Of course, Rabbi."

"We've found you an apartment," I told Mike one morning, as we were discussing the murder, by Imperial soldiers, of Hannah and her seven sons. "Isn't that wonderful? You can move in tomorrow."

"Excuse me Rov, what did you say?" He looked up at me. "I was engrossed by the tortuous spectacle of children dying for the glory of the Torah."

"We've found you an apartment," I said. "The committee. We're paying for it. It has heat, running water, a double bed, table, chairs, refrigerator, stove, closets, shelves, a bathroom, a fire alarm, even a television set with cable hook up. If you need anything else, we'll get that too. You can move tomorrow. I'll help you.

"Move?" he said, stunned. "But Rov, I can't leave. As I've told you, I'm the guardian, the Shomer. I must stand guard."

I smiled. "Mike, this is a real apartment with real amenities. Hot water, Mike. And it's clean—it's healthier for you. Look, I'll guard the synagogue. I can be the Shomer."

"No, Rov," he said excitedly, his eyes bulging. "Only I have the Mazel. I appreciate all of your concerns, but my expressive heart belongs in the attic. Away from here, I'm like the Jewish people without a land, like a dead soul with no resting place. Give the apartment back," he said, and looked back down at our text.

"Mike, Mike," I said. "You can't live here anymore. We've found you a real place, you can be comfortable." I touched his hand. "I'm sorry Mike." I said softly. "You have to move. I know you'll be happy there."

"I prophesy disaster," Mike said. "Only I can truly stand guard. Calamities will befall us."

"I'll help you move," I said.

"Disasters," he said.

The weekend after Mike moved out, the synagogue lost all electric power. I was in the middle of giving a sermon, on a steamy August night, when the lights, the air conditioner and the microphone all popped off at once. There was a slight sizzling from the microphone.

"It must be some kind of short," the custodian said. "Though I can't imagine why all of the lights would go out. The system is fairly new," he said, scratching his head, puzzled.

"I can't either." I said.

The lights were repaired just in time for the storm which blew off half of the synagogue's roof, and flooded most of the rooms.

"Well, Rabbi," said the synagogue president, "I guess we'll have to just replace the carpeting. I mean I don't think we'll ever get it really clean."

"I guess not." I said.

"Hopefully, we'll get the roof repaired by the High Holidays. Otherwise we'll just have to have services in the movie theatre." We paused to look up at the gaping hole in the ceiling. There were shreds of broken glass from blown out stain glass windows littering the damp carpet.

"Weird storm," he said. "I've been living here for thirty years, and I don't think I've ever seen a storm that freakish. Just came and went in a half hour. Strangest storm I've ever seen."

"Yes," I agreed. "It was freakish."

"Good thing our insurance was paid up."

"Yes," I said. "That is a good thing."

Had Mike caused the storm? Was he behind the power failure? I dismissed these nagging questions as paranoid superstitions. Mike was just some half-crazy homeless man with a Jewish background. Actually, he seemed fairly resigned to staying in his new apartment. He hardly complained at all. In fact we were still studying together at least once a week, though with all of the disasters, I had less time for him.

"We're going through a bit of bad luck," I explained to him one day, when he asked me about all of the water on the floor of my office.

"I see Rov," he said. "And my heart weeps for you, and your congregation. Really. But the luck will soon pass," he said. "Your wanderings will be over, your sanctuary repaired."

"Of course," I said.

"God is never angry forever," said Mike. "Even when His children betray Him to the false Gods, He stands ever ready to forgive, to forbear. So fear not, Rabbi Loeb, your sorrows will come to an end."

"Thank you Mike." I said. "How, uh, how do you like your new apartment?"

"Oh, it's quite nice," he said, smiling. "I especially enjoy the cable TV."

A week later, I received a phone call from the police. It was five thirty in the morning.

"Rabbi Loeb?" a voice said.

"Yes?" I said, sleepily.

"Sorry to wake you sir. There's a problem at the synagogue. I think you better get down here."

When I arrived, I found the inside and outside of the building covered with Anti-semitic graffiti. Big black gleaming swastikas shone out from the back wall of the auditorium. Blood red lightening strokes, symbols of the SS, blanketed the ceiling like red leprous patches on white skin. "Death to the Jews!" said the signs, and "Hitler was Right!" The entire front entrance of the building was smothered with yellow Jewish stars. It was ghastly. I stood gaping at the building, my mouth open, when the President arrived. He had tears in his eyes. We both stared at the building for a few minutes.

"Rabbi," he said finally, his voice trembling. "How on Earth . . . what could have happened?"

"Kids," I suggested. "A prank."

He shook his head. "Not kids, Rabbi. At least not young kids." He pointed to the graffiti. "Whoever painted that on, is at lest six feet tall, probably taller. Look how high up it is," he said. "Whoever did this is one tall man."

A tall man, I thought. Mike. I went to his apartment. I found him sitting on his sofa watching MTV. Used cans of spray paint were lying on the carpet.

"You accuse me?" he said, after I'd confronted him. "You have the nerve to suggest that I, even I, would vent my anger in such a disgusting manner. I whose only living thought is towards

God and His house. You, you rob the dead of their eternal resting home, you create exiles, you deface the name of God, you Rabbi Loeb." He stared at me, his eyes brimming with malice. "I've been watching TV all night," he said, and turned back to the screen.

"Mike!" I screamed. "Mike! The paint! The goddamn paint is right here, it's dripping on your rug. Red and yellow, Mike, like the graffiti." I picked up a can. "Black like the swastika."

He turned to me. "I was painting my car," he said. "I like those colors." he added.

"Mike," I said, still raising my voice. "Look, you need help. You probably don't even know what you're doing," I said, lowering my voice. He looked at me, a puzzled blank look in his eyes. I stared back at him for a few seconds, and gave up. I left his apartment and called the police. I told them I knew who had defaced the synagogue.

That night, after the police had taken Mike away, I dreamt that he and I were praying together at a synagogue in Jerusalem. He was the cantor, and I was the Rabbi. The sanctuary was in a cavernous room, holding hundreds of thousands of worshipers, all of them with their eyes directly trained on me and Mike. I announced the pages, and Mike, dressed in a beautiful flowing white robe, sang out with a melody so haunting and beautiful that tears formed in my eyes with each exquisite note. With his robe, and a fully grown dark red beard, Mike looked like King David himself, wailing out mournful psalms of the loss of the Temple and the destruction of Jerusalem. His voice, though achingly, relentlessly sad, was powerfully comforting as though its pain was full enough to absorb all the sadness in the world. We looked at him, the congregation and I, as a redeemer, someone whose strength could lead us back. I wanted to touch his robe, to feel his beard, to lose myself somehow in the power of his promise of redemption.

I woke up to the sounds of sirens. Fire engines were streaming down my block. I looked out my window, and I saw flames leaping up from the synagogue. The building was on fire. I threw on my bathrobe, and ran outside.

The building was small, and it was going up fast, the red flames shooting higher and higher. All I could do was stare while the fireman put up a futile battle to contain the fire. A crowd began to gather around the cordoned off area surrounding the building. Together we watched as the synagogue went up in smoke. Out of the corner of my eye, I saw Mike, in his grey wool suit, standing back a little from the crowd. He was looking at the synagogue with a deep grin on his face. The flames of the fire highlighted the red stubble of his beard. He was shaking a fist triumphantly at the doomed building, and shouting something in Hebrew. His eyes shone malignantly with all the storm, fury, and rage of a jealous God, avenging the exile of his people.

Not In Heaven

On that day R. Eliezer brought forward every imaginable argument, but they did not accept them. Said he to them: 'If the halachah agrees with me, let this carob-tree prove it!' Thereupon the carob-tree was torn a hundred cubits out of its place—others affirm, four hundred cubits. 'No proof can be brought from a carob-tree,' they retorted. Again he said to them: 'If the halachah agrees with me, let the stream of water prove it!' Whereupon the stream of water flowed backwards.—'No proof can be brought from a stream of water,' they rejoined. Again he urged: 'If the halachah agrees with me, let the walls of the schoolhouse prove it,' whereupon the walls inclined to fall. But R. Joshua rebuked them, saying: 'When scholars are engaged in a halachic dispute, what have ye to interfere?' Hence they did not fall, in honor of R. Joshua, nor did they resume the upright, in honor of R. Eliezer, and they are still standing thus inclined. Again he said to them: 'If the halachah agrees with me, let it be proved from Heaven!' Whereupon a Heavenly Voice cried out: 'Why do ye dispute with R. Eliezer, seeing that in all matters the halachah agrees with him!' But R. Joshua arose and exclaimed: 'It is not in heaven.'
—Talmud, Baba Metzia 59b

"Why can't you just drop it?" I say to my husband, the Rabbi. "Is it really all that important? It's just a stove," I point out. "After all."

He is angry, exasperated. "Haven't you been listening at all?" he says, loosening his tie while he paces around our living room. He looks out of our twentieth floor picture window with his powerful eyes, at the nighttime lights of Central Park. "It's not the goddamn stove—the stove is not the point. The point is how they ganged up on me. Especially your brother," he says accusingly, with a heavy accent on the word brother. "They're such witless fools, such imbeciles. They knew I was right—the stove is so obviously impure it bored the hell out of me to even repeat the argument. But that's not the point. The point is that I'm right, and your brother and his gang can't stand it. He's been after me ever since he became president. He's turned all the Rabbis against me, even my own students. Even Akiva." He paces some more, nearly wearing a groove in our new white carpet. He stares some more at the park.

53

"Sit down," I suggest hesitantly. I don't know quite what to say. He is difficult to handle when he is angry. He can be arrogant, mean. "Have a drink," I say.

Surprisingly, he does sit, plopping himself down on our blue Serta sofa bed. I hand him a club soda with just a touch of gin. He takes it gratefully, while twisting off his tie and tossing it on a chair. He, finally, is calm.

"I mean, I know I shouldn't get so worked up about it," he says quietly, "But it is my job. And the oven is so obviously impure—the arguments for purity were such fluff, such nonsense. Not really arguments at all. But Gamliel has them in the palm of his hand—he's a goddamn dictator. 'Majority rule,' he says. 'We follow the majority.' The arrogant schmuck. They follow him. He's pissed off because I won't go along."

I sit down next to him, take his hand. I sense his outrage reigniting.

"But the worst part is how blind they are. Willfully blind. I was so sure I was right, I was willing to risk everything—I put my whole spiritual reputation on the line." He is trembling. "Shhh," I say, stroking his arm, but he's up again and pacing.

"I risked everything," he says, storming across the room. "I put it on the line. I said, 'Look, if I'm right let that big Oak tree in Riverside park—the one right outside our window—jump ten feet in the air.' And it did, Goddammit, I swear! It jumped ten feet in the air! Someone said it jumped forty feet! But they said—those schmucks—'trees don't prove anything.' So I said, 'All right, if I'm right, let the Hudson flow backwards.' And, I swear to God it did. We looked out the window, and it was flowing the other way! The entire Hudson River! Boats, big ships were moving backwards! But they said, those detestable sycophants, 'Rivers don't prove anything.' So I said—you understand I was beginning to lose patience?"

I understood.

"I said let the walls of this building prove I'm right! And the walls—I'm not kidding—all of the walls, the four walls—tilted inside thirty degrees! The whole building nearly collapsed! It was like we were in a goddamn tepee! Of course Joshua, that nebbish, pushed them up again, but even he couldn't get them up all the way. They were still tilted when I left this afternoon, I doubt they'll ever straighten them out."

He stops at the window and peers out. We listen to sirens roaring down Central Park West. He turns to look at me, his eyes open wide.

"So I give them the ultimate guarantee. Trees don't impress them, the river doesn't impress them, the building means nothing to those idiots—I decide to go all the way. I say 'If I'm right, let heaven itself prove it. Heaven itself!' And, Emma, I swear to you, I swear to God, a voice from Heaven fills up the room! A voice from the sky! God's voice! And it says, 'Rabbi Eliezer is right! The oven is impure!' Now, even Gamliel, your insufferably tyrannical brother is impressed. They're all shocked—for once in their lives, they're speechless. They heard it! Heaven proved me right! But then Joshua—that fake, that arrogant phony—Gamliel's pet, his stooge—he gets up and talks back to the voice—back to God. He says, with that horribly pious, nasal whine—'It's not in Heaven.' "

He pauses.

"It's not in Heaven," he repeats scornfully, staring out the window. "What the hell is that supposed to mean? Not in Heaven? What's not in Heaven?" he shakes his head. "I'd had enough. I got out of there." He sits back on the couch. With one gulp, he finishes his drink. We sit in silence for a few moments. Finally he takes the remote control and turns on CNN. We watch the news.

I worry about Eliezer. A brilliant man—a compassionate man—but so high strung—so temperamental. So much like my brother Gamliel. I remember when we met. My brother brought him home one night for dinner. They were both starting guards on the basketball team at Yeshiva University High School in Los Angeles. I remember being utterly smitten at their tall lean bodies—covered with sweat—fresh from basketball practice. I'd always had a crush on my brother, a crush which I frankly admit bordered on the forbidden. I loved to watch him work out—to stretch his taut but substantial thigh and calf muscles before he would go for a six mile run. I adored him—his intellect, his sense of humor, his scathing wit, and his body—yes, his body. But of course I was foolish—it was a school girl crush like the one I had on my kindergarten teacher at Beis Ya'akov, a lovely young rebetzin with long brown hair. I loved my brother deeply, much more than I loved my mother—a shy heavy set woman never really comfortable with children, or my father—a tyrannical Rosh Yeshiva with no use for women. My brother was my only real source of family love—my only experience with real kindness. But I could never want him—I knew that—from an early age I knew that. But I could want Eliezer—and, from nearly the first moment I saw him—I did.

I was only nineteen when we married. He was twenty four—already a renowned Rabbi—a boy wonder. Naturally, I was a virgin, eager and nervous. We made love three times on our wedding night, and once in the morning. It was thrilling, liberating. Yet I was filled with shame. Each time, right before I reached orgasm, I thought of Gamliel. The last time, in the blessed early hours of the morning after, a picture of his bearded face filled my brain like a vision. I had to stop myself from screaming. I held on tightly to Eliezer's lean back and tried to love him strongly. But the vision of Gamliel frightened me. By age thirty, Eliezer and Gamliel were both appointed to the Sanhedrin in New York. Gamliel, nearly as brilliant as Eliezer, was by far the better politician. Five years after our move to the Upper West Side of Manhattan, Gamliel was made president of the Sanhedrin. It was then they began to drift apart—the two men I loved most in the world. Eliezer chafed under Gamliel's dictatorial restructuring of the Sanhedrin; no one had ever led the Rabbis with such a heavy hand. Eliezer, secure in his own brilliance, could not imagine ever taking instruction in Torah from the smoother Gamliel. They quarreled—respectfully at first—but later violently, emotionally. Eliezer was by far the more sensitive of the two. After a stormy session with his former friend—my brother—he would come home, rail at Gamliel, have a drink, and at night, in bed, cry softly. His tears burned holes in our pillows.

I worry, because I know what could happen. Eliezer has become unpopular with his colleagues. He has not been able to control his temper. Lately his rulings in his own court have seemed harsh, sometimes even cruel. Last week he shocked even his most dedicated students by insisting that the biblical precept 'an eye for an eye,' was meant literally—and not, as we have come to understand, as a metaphor for monetary compensation. No one understands the origins of this new hard heartedness—people are suggesting that he may be going insane. Only I know the reason. He is hurt that his friend Gamliel, my brother, should treat him so disrespectfully—so disdainfully. This effects his judgment. He is so sensitive.

There has been talk of excommunication. Akiva, Eliezer's former student, whispers the word to me on Saturday night, when we run into him at the *Godfather III*. Joshua's wife hints at it to me on Sunday when I take our children ice skating at Paine pavilion. She tells me they are considering 'blessing' my husband. She uses a euphemism; she cannot even bare to say the word. They—the Sanhedrin—Eliezer's colleagues—are considering imposing the ultimate disgrace, the ultimate shame. Excommunication. And Eliezer is so tender, so sensitive. I worry about him, he will take it badly. And I worry about my brother Gamliel.

One night it happens. Suddenly Akiva is in our apartment, appearing out of the blue, unannounced by our doorman. He is dressed entirely in black; he is wearing a black leather jacket, black jeans, and the black tennis shoes he uses on Yom Kippur and Tisha B'av. He even appears to have dyed his beard a darker shade of black—it nearly glistens—shining, reflecting under the light of our lamps. His face is grim, he is pained. Akiva, a prominent Rabbi in his own right, has been Eliezer's most loyal, most loving student. Now he has death in his eyes.

"It seems," he says, almost whispering, his voice hoarse. This is not easy for him. "It seems, my teacher, that your friends have separated themselves from you."

"Excommunication?" Eliezer says softly, almost matter of factly, as if he had been expecting it.

Akiva nods.

"I see," says my husband. He looks down. He is still standing tall, his proud body has not yet absorbed the blow. "You should leave," he says to Akiva. He does. Eliezer winces at the slamming of the door. "Gamliel," he says softly, his low voice filled with hate and humiliation. "Gamliel has finally done it." He shakes his head. "The shame," he whispers. "The shame." He looks up at the door. Tears form in his eyes and stream down his cheeks. They fall on the rug, and burn holes in our carpet.

My husband has powers. I've known this since we've been married. His sorrow can be destructive. His tears can be like acid—burning and destroying whatever they touch. He is so sensitive. I've had to replace sheets, pillows—sew patches into his bathrobe. I once injured my hand brushing away a tear from his cheek. He is not aware of his power, but I am. I fear that power now—now that his life has been shattered.

I have visions—fearsome, frightening visions. While cleaning the stove or vacuuming or shopping I am halted suddenly with a vision of my brother Gamliel. I seem him dropping dead of a heart attack, his shaking hand desperately clutching at his chest, tearing at his shirt, his face contorted in pain as he falls to the ground. I know that this is absurd. Gamliel, at age forty is in terrific shape. He still jogs six miles a day around Central Park, and plays handball on Sundays. His cholesterol level is in the safest possible category, his blood pressure has been low for years. He is the least likely candidate for a heart attack. Yet I see him dying, leaving behind a wife and three young children. And a grieving sister. The night Akiva gave us the news, as Eliezer and I were making love, as I slowly came to orgasm, I received my first vision. Gamliel's funeral. His children crying. His wife pale and sick behind her black veil.

A few days later, Eliezer and I are having breakfast on our terrace overlooking the West Side. He is morose, bereft like a man in mourning. He has not shaved in days, and his grayish stubble makes him look old. He sips his orange juice in silence and stares out across the city.

"I see an airplane," he whispers.

I look up. I have been reading the paper, an article on the inner life of Saddam Hussein. "Pardon me?" I ask.

He gestures toward the east with his head. I see a white plane, high in the sky, whizzing past our apartment. "I see that airplane quite clearly," he says. "I can't seem to take my eyes off of it."

I, too, stare at the plane. Suddenly, I have another vision. I see Gamliel in the cabin of the airplane. I see the fasten seat belts signs light up suddenly. I see the entire aircraft lurch to the right and then to the left, Gamliel grabbing on to his seat to avoid being thrown. Trays of food are flying through the narrow corridor. I see panic in the faces of the passengers and the stewardesses. I hear screams. I see oxygen masks being released, alarms sounding, the plane listing, heading toward a crash landing.

Eliezer is still staring. "Look away!" I say sharply. He continues to stare as if in a trance. "Look away!" I yell.

The shrillness of my voice surprises him. He looks at me, finally breaking off his skyward gaze. "Why?" he asks.

I exhale deeply. The vision disappears. The next day, I discover that, enroute to an interfaith conference in Buffalo, Gamliel's plane nearly crashed. It was saved at the last minute by the nearly miraculous intervention of the co-pilot.

Even as young men, Gamliel and Eliezer competed for my attention. When I went to their basketball games, they would leap over each other to perform some act of court daring—always looking up in the stands to make sure that I had noticed. After the game, they would fight to open the car door for me, fight to sit next to me at the restaurant, fight for who would get the honor of paying the bill. There was, of course, humor as well as chivalry, in this battle. And I revelled in the competition. But there was a sober kind of seriousness that lurked in the back recesses of our triad—a tension which insinuated its way into our happiness like a snake. Gamliel couldn't let go of me as a sister. And I was not sure I wanted to be let go. I loved Eliezer, I loved Gamliel. I adore him. I love Gamliel too much.

I worry, now, that he will die. Eliezer's shame runs deep, it pervades everything he does. Since the airplane incident, I fear his power more than ever. He laughs at me, calls me foolish—superstitious. But I stare at the holes in our pillow cases, the small round wounds in our rug. I know the power of grief, of humiliation. Eliezer is a beaten man. He will stop at nothing.

I have a vision. I see Gamliel's two blond daughters visiting his tombstone. They have grown up, they are young adults. They are weeping uncontrollably. The grave is nicely kept, tidy and colorful with flowers, but it is a gray, cold day. In my vision, I can almost feel the chill of the winter wind which sweeps down on the two grieving women. Snow begins to fall. In the corner of the vision, far in the distance, I see Eliezer. It's impossible to see him clearly. But I sense that he is smiling.

I forbid him to say the Tahanun prayers—prayers of sorrow and mourning. They are too powerful, I tell him—the impact of their grief will harm Gamliel. He chuckles—cannot imagine where I acquired these fears—but he humors me. He promises that he will forego the daily Tahanun prayers—the prayers where one prostrates oneself before God—as long as I demand it. I will demand it for some time. In fact, I don't trust him. I stay with him each morning, and each afternoon to make sure he skips Tahanun. If he begins to fall on his face in supplication, I reach out and grab him. I pull on his powerful biceps until he stands completely erect. He laughs. He calls it foolishness. But I am serious.

Time passes. Eliezer seems to heal. He still reads and studies. He plays basketball twice a week at the Y. He is eating well, taking care of himself. He had begun writing a novel. He is considering accepting a tenure-track offer to teach Jewish studies at Columbia. We make love at least twice a week, as often as I talk to my brother Gamliel on the phone. My visions have nearly gone away. Yet I am vigilant. I watch my husband's eyes, guard his meditations. I pray with him every day, mouth the Hebrew words along with him, and make sure he skips the mournful penitential prayers. Eliezer tells me that he has forgiven Gamliel. That he is happier away from the rough and tumble world of Sanhedrin politics. He is getting more work done than ever before, he says. He would never harm Gamliel, he would sooner hurt himself. He is, after all—he says—his brother-in-law. But I watch.

One day I wake up late, For some reason my alarm has not gone off. I bolt up in a panic, and run into Eliezer's study. I am relieved. He is just now fastening his black tefillin on to his upper arm, and has not yet even begun the introductory prayers. He nods at me, smiling a little, and turns to his small prayerbook. I calculate that I have at least twenty minutes before Tahanun. The door bell rings, an unusual sound in our apartment. Normally the doorman announces any visitor, and I leave the door open. I exchange glances with Eliezer, and hurry to answer the bell.

It is a homeless man, a beggar. I recognize him; he usually stands on the corner of Lexington and 59th, where I get off the bus everyday for work. He is a tall, good natured (under the circumstances) black man who almost always—inexplicably—greets me in the morning with a word of Yiddish or Hebrew.

He hold out a cup. "Some change?" he asks nicely.

I am confused. How did he get in?

"Some change?" he asks again. "It's for food," he adds. He waits patiently, jingling his cup of change.

I search frantically through the pockets of my house coat, looking for quarters or dimes. He waits, holding a lit cigarette in his free hand. Again, he shakes his cup. I hurry into our bedroom, rummage through the subway tokens and bobby pins in the top drawer of my dresser, and—finally—find two quarters and a dime. I grab the change and run back to the door. He is gone. I peer down the hallway, but I don't see him. A faint odor of cigarette smoke is noticeable near the entrance to the apartment. But the man is gone. I think that perhaps he has snuck into the apartment. I look in the kitchen—there is no sign of him. I give up.

I remember Eliezer. My heart starts beating wildly, and I run into his study. I am too late. He is lying face down in a prone position, supplicating before God. He is trembling vigorously, and I can hear him choking back sobs.

"Get up!" I yell. "For God's sake Eliezer, get up!"

He pays no attention. He is shaking, vibrating, beating his fist into the rug. "Get up!" I scream—I yell with all my might. I am hysterical.

He stops. Slowly, he rises and looks at me. He frightens me; there is a chill of satisfaction in his eyes, or revenge—long put off—but suddenly satisfied. It is like death, like murder. We look at each other. Together, we hear the roar of an ambulance rushing past our building. The phone rings. I let it go for three rings then carefully pick up the receiver. I look at Eliezer. He is smiling like a demon. I hear the news. I scream.

The Day the Temple Burned Down

Judah came to see me in the middle of April, right before Passover. In fact, he was my last appointment before my vacation; I always make it a point to take off the week of Passover. At first I didn't recognize him. That in itself wasn't surprising, it had been twenty years since we'd seen each other at our high school graduation and we'd both changed quite a bit, neither of us, I'm afraid, for the better. I was surprised, however, that I didn't even recognize his name. Judah and I had been friends in high school—on occasion close friends. And his name—Judah Loev—isn't exactly run of the mill. I would have thought that his name on my calendar would have at least rung a bell. But I had no idea who he was—an old pal from Cleveland Heights, Ohio—until he told me.

Before we got down to business, we spent a few minutes reminiscing. Oddly, the stories he brought up were things I'd forgotten. He reminded me of prom night, how a group of us had driven down to Shaker Lakes to watch the sun rise, and how my date—my high school sweetheart Michelle—had abandoned me for Bob Packer—a football player. When he told me the story, I remembered it clearly—as if it were yesterday. But until that moment I'd forgotten all about it. He also reminded me of my three week summer affair with Joan Gross at Camp Anisfield, which ended when Joan's real boyfriend visited from Israel. I suppose it wouldn't be accurate to say that I'd forgotten all about Joan, or about how devastated I was by the whole episode. But before Judah had mentioned her name, I can't say that I'd thought about her—or Camp Anisfield, for that matter—for over fifteen years.

Finally, I asked him why he had come to see me. He told me that, in some ways, he'd just as soon spend the hour talking about old times. He suspected that reminiscing with an old friend might be therapy enough. I encouraged him, in any case, to tell me the problem.

This was it. He was having vibrant, crystal clear memories of an event that he couldn't possibly have experienced.

"What event?" I asked.

"The destruction of the second Temple in Jerusalem," he said. "In the year 70 c.e." he added.

He remembered, he told me, the powerful heat of the fires,

the guttural Hebrew curses of the Jewish soldiers, the smell of the burning wood, the sight of sweat glistening on the cheeks of Roman centurions. He remembered it all, he informed me, not *as if* he were there, but—seemingly—*because*—he was there. And, he was quick to tell me, I shouldn't confuse this with a kind of mystical vision, or a past life experience, or some kind of fleeting psychotic episode. He remembered it because he *lived through* it—there in Jerusalem, though of course he couldn't really have lived through it, since it happened almost two thousand years before he was born.

"When did you first realize that you had this memory?" I asked him, taking out my notepad and pencil.

He thought for a moment, pondering—it seemed to me—whether or not he should really tell me the whole story. Finally, he shrugged and said, "Two years ago, on Tisha B'av."

Tisha B'av is the ninth day of the Hebrew month of Av—the day the temple was destroyed, and a day of fasting and mourning in the Jewish calendar. It made psychological sense that Judah's delusion would begin on that day. I looked at him, waiting for him to elaborate.

"I was in *schull*, for services," he said. "The lights were off and we were sitting on the floor. There were candles burning all around us. You know the custom?"

In fact I don't, but nodded anyway.

"Then the *chazen* started chanting *eichah*—the book of Lamentations. It's such a haunting melody—so plaintive and lovely. I listened to him for a few moments, I was even swaying a little, back and forth, back and forth, and—suddenly—these memories started rushing through my head. I remembered an incident as if it was yesterday. I was eight years old. I was lying on some straw in a one-room stone house, trying to sleep. Suddenly the whole place started to fill up with smoke. My parents started shouting and grabbing dishes, plates, food—whatever they could—and hustling me out of the house. We ran through curvy, stone-paved streets. Hundreds of people were fleeing with us, jabbering in Aramaic, or Hebrew—I wasn't sure which. We ended up in a courtyard on top of a hill, where we had a panoramic view of almost the whole city. I could see a huge golden building being completely consumed by flames. Somehow I knew it was the temple. Everyone around me stared straight ahead at the fire. And then everyone started crying. I cried too, I cried my eyes out. In fact, I think I remember the crying more than anything else."

He looked at me. "That's it," he said, and shrugged again. "But like I said, this was no dream. I wasn't asleep. This was a memory!"

"Has this happened again?" I asked. "This sudden flooding of your mind with these memories?"

"Oh, yeah, yeah," he answered. "It happens a lot. One time I heard a song on the radio that had almost the same melody as that *chazen's* chanting. The memories rushed in. Another time I saw a school burning on the news. It happened again."

"And in between these flashes," I asked. "Do you still 'remember' this incident? Without the stimuli? Do you remember it right now?"

"Eric," he said. "I remember it completely. In every detail."

"You mean you remember the vision of it? You remember the experience at the *schull* on Tisha B'av?"

"No, no," he insisted, with some impatience. "I remember myself as a little boy. Watching, while our holy temple is going up in smoke. I remember it happening to me. It's as clear to me as . . . as . . . as that time in ninth grade cooking class when Mrs. Jacobson made the two of us go home and take baths because she said we smelled."

"Pardon me?" I asked. At first I didn't know what he was talking about. But even as he began filling in the details of that particularly mortifying episode, it all came back to me. It was our freshman year of high school. Judah and I had spent the previous period—a study hall—running laps around the football field. We had delusions of making the track team. It was a wet drizzly day, and we both stumbled several times. By the end of the period we were thoroughly muddy—which we noticed—but also fairly rank—which, for some reason, we didn't notice. We managed to find a hose, but all we could do was spread the dirt around our clothes. We showed up to class damp, dirty, and—apparently—smelling like a cow field. Mrs. Jacobson, one of our more sadistic teachers, paraded us in front of our fellow students—among them Kathy Young, a girl I'd had a crush on for over a year—and sent us home. It was a deeply humiliating experience, but for some reason I'd forgotten all about it.

Judah and I agreed on a schedule for therapy, he'd see me once a week, starting the week after Passover. I wasn't entirely clear what the purpose of the therapy would be. Judah told me that he wanted "to be normal." It obviously wasn't "normal" to remember something—especially in such a vivid way—that couldn't possibly have happened. It was a symptom of neurosis. But Judah didn't seem neurotic in any significant way. He held down a steady job, was happily married, had two kids. The temple memories didn't fill him with panic or anxiety; he wasn't even sure he wanted them to go away. He just wanted to understand them. I told him I would help him try.

Judah was my last patient of the day. I held out his coat to him, and walked with him to his car. As we shook hands and said goodbye—wishing each other a pleasant holiday—he looked, just for an instant, deeply into my eyes. His gaze startled me, it seemed haunted, suddenly morose and filled with foreboding.

Startled, and a little frightened, I turned away.

In my own car, driving home—coincidentally—I heard a James Taylor song which had been popular my senior year of high school. I was about to turn it off—I despise sappy folk music—when something in the melody jogged my memory. I had a sudden flash once again of prom night, of Shaker Lakes, and my date—Michelle Cydulka. I had a kind of vision of her talking to me, maybe even laughing at me, but I couldn't recall exactly what she was saying. In fact, I couldn't get a clear image of her facial expression. I only know that whatever she said and did hurt me deeply. I felt an immense sadness sweep through me, a nearly incapacitating wave of regret and grief—more intense than anything I'd ever felt as an adult, let alone as a love-stricken adolescent. I almost had to pull over and stop the car, but, fortunately, the feeling left me as quickly as it had arrived. I drove on, letting the song play for a few more moments before switching to a classical music station.

"It happened again," Judah said, as soon as he walked in for our next meeting. I motioned for him to sit down.

"What happened?" I asked.

"Another memory flash," he said. "Fire, mad panic, Roman soldiers—the whole scene. It all came rushing back." He described to me the memory. He was back in ancient Israel, on the hill overlooking Jerusalem where his family had found refuge after fleeing their house. He and his "parents" ran down the hill towards the city, apparently hoping to help put out the fires and maybe even save the Temple. It sounded like a particularly harrowing scene. Judah's father was hit in the foot by a spear, and then trampled by a horse. He appeared to die, though Judah couldn't remember exactly. He also lost track of his mother in the crowd.

"The last thing I remember," he told me. "Was wandering off myself back to our stone house. I thought maybe I'd find my mother there. But I can't remember what happened next." He shrugged and smiled. He seemed strangely cheerful despite these dreadful memories.

"What set off the memory?" I asked. "What was the stimulus?"

"It was a James Taylor song," he said.

"Pardon me?"

He shrugged again. "There's a line about fire in it—the sky being on fire—something like that. I guess it made me think about burning and smoke and—well, there it was. I was back in Jerusalem, watching the temple burn." He smiled again. "Funny," he said. "Now that I think of it, that was the song that was playing on the radio when you were bashing your head against the mirror in our high school bathroom."

"What on earth . . . ?"

"You remember," he said. "The day after prom. You were so depressed, I think you were trying to kill yourself with the glass. I had to call the security . . ."

"That never happened!" I shouted, interrupting. But even as I said it, I began to remember. The blood flowing down my cheeks. The purple bruise on my forehead. The warm, earthy embrace of the security guards as they dragged me out of the bathroom. Crying in the guidance counselor's arms. It did happen; I had just forgotten. But how could I ever had done something like that?

Judah looked at me, concerned. But I was already calming down. We dropped the subject of our high school days, and spent the rest of the hour talking about Judah's relationship with his parents.

"I ran all the way down the hill, past the city gates. Everything was in complete chaos. Soldiers barking orders, women wailing, people bleeding. I couldn't run for two feet without seeing a dead body." This was our next session. Judah was describing for me a further memory flash. It had come to him that morning, after he'd cut himself shaving. "Of course, everyone just ignored me. I was only eight years old. And I wasn't saying a word. Anyhow, I ran out of the city and down towards some kind of stream. I remember I was dying of thirst, and I thought if I could just get to the water. I finally made it, but the area around the stream was covered with refugees, all filling up jugs with water. The stream itself looked filthy, muddy and filled with sediment. But I didn't care. I wiggled my way through the crowd, and jumped into the stream. I opened my mouth and just let the water pour in. Of course, when you do that, you can't breathe, you start to drown. And that's what happened." He looked at me, a slight grin on his face.

"You drowned?" I asked.

"No, no," he said. "Of course not. I *started* to drown. But some of the people—the refugees—pulled me out of the water just in time. They dragged me to the edge of the stream and started to . . . well they took me and . . ." He stopped, wrinkled his brow, and then shrugged. "Actually," he said. "I don't remember what happened next." He smiled and then shrugged again. "But I'm sure it will come to me."

"I'm sure." I said.

"It's funny though, isn't it? That I remember about almost drowning? Now, just when you and I have become re-acquainted? Now, of all times, I suddenly have a memory of drowning? Don't you think that's funny?"

"What," I said slowly. "Are you talking about?"

"Well, probably my most intense memory of high school—I

mean the thing that I will *never* forget—is that time you tried to drown Bob Packer in the swimming pool. I mean it was just so . . ."

"What?!" I yelled out, practically leaping out of my chair. I felt myself losing control. The blood rushed to my face. I balled my hands into fists.

"Now, calm down Eric. I just . . ."

"That is simply not true! I could never . . ."

"It *is* true, Eric, If I hadn't . . ."

"Get out Judah." I said. I was suddenly filled with tremendous anger. I was furious at his lies, at his malicious, hurtful 'memories.' I needed for him to disappear. I walked over to him, feeling as if I could punch, or even strangle him. "Get out!" I screamed.

He fled.

But that night I remembered it. Actually, I dreamt about it. Packer, Judah and I were hanging around the pool after swim class. The bell rang, but none of us was ready to head to the locker room and change. Packer had to tell me something. Judah stayed behind. I'm not sure why; I guess for moral support.

Packer towered over me. With his bulging football-star muscles, he made me feel puny, midget-like. He shoved his fingers in my face and started screaming at me. He looked like a demon with his beet-red cheeks, and wide opened green eyes. He shouted and shouted at me, but I couldn't understand a word he was saying; I'm not sure I could even hear him. But he sparked a fury in me, vicious and blazing. I hated him with every fiber of my being; I felt it in my stomach, I hated him so much it hurt. Jealousy and rage ran through my blood like black bile, driving me practically insane. I kicked his legs out from under him, sending him crashing into the pool. Diving in after him, I grabbed his hair and—while keeping it under water—shoved his head up against the pool wall. The pupils of his eyes moved to the back of his head, and I saw blood coloring the water around his forehead. I knew I was killing him. I didn't care. I was about to kick his eyes, when I felt Judah grab me from behind and drag me out of the pool.

I woke up from the dream panting, and in a cold sweat. I forced open a window, and ran to the bathroom for some water. I took several deep breaths, trying to relax. I told myself that it was only a dream—that none of it really happened. But I knew that wasn't true. It was a dream, but it did happen. I'd just forgotten all about it.

I also knew that there was a lot more that I still hadn't remembered. What had happened to Bob Packer? Was he seriously hurt, and—if so—what were the consequences to me? Was I suspended, arrested? Beaten up? I couldn't remember. I had a vague, unpleasant feeling that the incident in the pool was just the beginning of something really horrible that happened later that month. But, for the life of me, I couldn't recall a single detail. Except for one. I was pretty sure it had something to do with Judah.

The next day, I found Judah sitting at my chair, his feet propped up on my desk. My secretary, who for seven years always arrived fifteen minutes before me, was nowhere to be seen. I set down my briefcase and sat on the couch. Judah was staring at the ceiling. For a split second he looked to me exactly like the youthful Judah of our high school years. But I quickly noticed the grey in his hair, the wrinkles on his forehead. He'd gotten older.

"It was because of our sins," he said.

I nodded.

"That's why our holy temple burned to the ground. That's why we were thrown into Exile. The Lord vented all His fury, poured out His blazing wrath; He kindled a fire in Zion which consumed its foundations. It was for the sins of her prophets, the iniquities of her priests who had shed in her midst the blood of the just." He looked at me. "Am I making myself clear?" he asked.

"I'm remembering it all very clearly now, Eric," he said. "It wasn't a stream outside of Jerusalem. That's not it at all. We were by the waters of Babylon. There we wept. The wicked carried us away. How can we sing a song to God in a strange land? I remember it all now." He stopped talking for a moment while he kicked off his shoes. I noticed there were holes in his socks.

"Because of our sins, we were exiled from our land. It's all coming back to me, you see, I see it all now, I know exactly what happened. We all knew it. God was punishing us, God was becoming our enemy, because we sinned. As we marched into exile, we all knew it, we cried about it. On the other hand, we were confident the exile wouldn't last forever. All we had to do was pay for our sins. Then God would take us back. That's what we told each other along the way." He started whistling, a strange mournful melody that sounded like something I'd heard a long time ago at the synagogue. On the other hand, it might have been an old James Taylor tune; I wasn't sure.

"Judah," I said.

"Shhh!" Don't interrupt. You need to hear this. The only way we could end the exile was to pay for our sins. That was absolutely clear in our minds. And that's what you need to know. You can end your exile when you wipe out *your* sin."

He swung his feet around and faced me directly. I was momentarily startled. Suddenly—for just a moment—it wasn't Judah facing me at all. It was Bob Packer, with a wide gash

67

across his forehead. But it must have been an illusion, or a trick of the light; a moment later it was the same old Judah.

"End your exile, Eric," he said. "Pay for your sins. It's the only way."

I shook my head. "I don't know what you're talking about."

He came out from behind the desk and grinned. He tried to touch my shoulder, but I recoiled. Instead he leaned into my ear and whispered softly. "Admit what you did," he said as his surprisingly sweet smelling, damp breath enveloped my entire face. "And this can end. The destruction. The alienation. We can all go back. Like dreamers, Eric, we can be like dreamers. Song can fill our mouth. But you have to pay for your sin. Pay for what you did."

I was about to push him away, when he jerked his head up, smiled again, and walked out the door. I followed after him to see if my secretary had returned. She was sitting in her usual spot, though for a moment I could have sworn that it was not her at all, but an adult version of my old girlfriend Michelle. But, of course, I was mistaken.

What had I done? What was my sin? That I had beat the shit out of Bob Packer and almost drowned him? That certainly wasn't pleasant of me, yet I didn't think that could be it, oddly, it seemed to me that he had deserved it. It wasn't an act that *felt* at all sinful, not to me. That night, as I was trying to relax, watching another rerun of "Star Trek: The Next Generation," I suddenly had a nagging feeling that it had something to do with Michelle. I had done something to Michelle, something serious—even more serious than slamming Bob Packer's head into the side of a swimming pool. Or had I?

I went to sleep that night expecting to dream about Michelle. That had been the pattern so far. Judah would remind me of some event, I would deny that it ever occurred, and then I would either remember it all in a flash—the memories cascading through my brain—or I would dream about it. Judah was my memory catalyst, all I had to do was wait a day or two after talking to him and my past became apparent. But it didn't happen that night, at least not in the way I'd expected it to. I woke up early, almost an hour before dawn, but I couldn't remember any of my dreams, though I knew that I'd had at least a dozen, all about high school. I had a feeling Michelle played a starring role in each of the dreams, but it was only a feeling—I had no direct memory of even seeing her face. In fact, as I lay in bed, my eyes glued to the ceiling, I couldn't form any coherent image in my mind of Michelle at all. I'd forgotten what she looked like.

I turned on the nightstand lamp, and fumbled through the bookcase until I found my high school yearbook. I took a deep breath and opened it, somehow turning right to the page with her picture. She looked at me, smiling broadly—her braces-free teeth (she'd had them removed the week before) gleaming brightly back at the camera. I looked at the picture for several minutes until, without warning, tears started to leak out of my eyes. I was crying, but I didn't know why. Suddenly, I gasped. A red streak appeared across Michelle's cheek, as if she'd been cut. I was about to scream out loud when I realized that one of my tears had fallen on the picture and—mixed with the other colors on the page—had created the illusion of blood pouring off of her face.

I couldn't go to work. I was afraid Judah would show up. In any case I was exhausted. I phoned my secretary and had her cancel all my appointments for a week. The next several nights I had the same dreams: all about high school, all staring Michelle (and myself). And, upon awaking—always near dawn—I couldn't remember a single detail. I spent entire days doing nothing but studying my year book, memorizing names, dates, pictures. I recited to myself the names of the members of the debate club, the swimming club, the outing club. I became entirely familiar with the records of the basketball team, football team, lacrosse team, tennis team, and learned—by heart—the personal statistics of every member of the baseball team and the women's soccer team. I re-learned the names of all the teachers, in all the departments. I memorized the office structure. Principal—David Decarlo (a heavy set man with thinning gray hair), Vice Principal—Ann Lerner (a strict disciplinarian with a stern face and an incongruously squeaky high voice), senior class guidance counselor—Ron Malone, registrar—Emily Pierce. I studied the faces of all of my classmates—their pimples, greasy hair, their beauty marks, braces, and tie-died shirts, their breasts, their eyes. I did all this with one particular goal in mind. I hoped that something in the book might jog my memory, that I might finally recall that dreadful sin that—according to Judah—sent me into exile. But nothing worked. The same painful, dreary pattern occurred over and over again. The vague dreams, the early dawn awakenings, and the daily journey through the melancholy minutia of Cleveland Heights High School. But no real memories.

One early morning—it was the beginning of August—after the usual sweaty night of inconclusive dreaming, I began to suspect that my answer could only be found there—back in Cleveland Heights. If I was in exile, maybe the answer was to go back home. I thought for a moment and realized that I hadn't been home in seven years, since my mother's funeral. I was momentarily stunned. How could so much time have gone by? I picked up my yearbook—like an amulet, it now occupied a permanent place on my nightstand—and looked up my own picture. I was struck at how trouble-free my face appeared,

69

considering all the turbulence of my senior year. I was smiling widely; I looked almost happy. And young, so very young. I put down the book and looked at my own face in the mirror. My hair was almost entirely gray. My face was rounding out. I saw lines on my forehead, wrinkles around the eyes. Too much time had passed. I made a reservation to fly to Cleveland the next day.

I was filled with dread driving to the airport, and several times almost turned around. But on the airplane I actually began to look forward to seeing Cleveland again. Settling into my seat with a drink, it occurred to me that my high school experience was really not all that bad. I'd fallen in love for the first time, had my first tentative, groping experience with sex. I also realized that—even though I was no longer in touch with anyone—my high school friendships were the most intense and satisfying of my life. As the airplane engines lulled me into an almost hypnotic trance, pleasant memories—like storybook freight trains—began rolling into my mind. Nothing special or dramatic—just some good times. Playing basketball, eating at McDonalds. Learning to drive. Listening to rock music. I even thought a little about Michelle. Our time together, I realized, was the happiest time of my life. And if it ended badly, that was still no reason to dismiss the whole experience, and certainly no reason to regard my high school years with horror.

The horror, it occurred to me, had only entered my consciousness after Judah reappeared in my life. But he was crazy, I told myself, that was absolutely clear now. I should know. And I'd let his craziness somehow turn my life upside down. How did I let that happen, I wondered, how could I have let a patient's problems (and let's face it, Judah was just a patient. He'd stopped being a friend year ago) seep into my own consciousness and even threaten my hold on sanity? As the plane flew closer to my old home town, I felt the influence of Judah's madness fade. I felt better than I had in weeks. I looked forward to seeing my old house, where I'd grown up, my old suburban neighborhood. Maybe I'd look up some old friends. Visit the high school.

Shortly before landing, I had a dream; not a memory, not a vision, just a dream. I was in ancient Jerusalem, wandering through the remains of the Temple. Smoke danced off of the still smoldering, black ruin. I saw pilgrims on the horizon, dressed in black cloaks. They were chanting a haunting—achingly beautiful—wordless tune which seemed vaguely familiar. I walked up to them, and recognized the melody; it was the synagogue chant for the book of Lamentations. But when I got closer, somehow it changed into an old James Taylor tune. And I saw the pilgrims—singing with desperate sadness, as if it were the ruins of their own lives abandoned in smoking decay along the hill—were none other than my high school mates: Michelle, Bob Packer, and Judah Loev.

At the airport, I rented a car and headed for Cleveland Heights. I thought to myself that I would first drive to the house where I grew up, the house my father sold after his wife died and he moved to Florida. I figured I would pull in the driveway, peek in the window, maybe even gather up the nerve to ring the doorbell and wander around inside. Then, I thought, I would have lunch at Corky and Saul's—the deli my friends and I used to patronize on Friday nights after basketball games. After that, I would find a hotel, check in, and possibly take a nap for an hour or two. Only then, I decided, would I head for the high school and . . . do what? I wasn't sure. Have a look around, I imagined. Maybe try to find my old locker.

That, at least, was the plan. But as soon as I turned on to I70 and headed east, I knew that I was going to go straight to the high school, with no stops in between. I was not surprised to find that—even though it had been twenty years—I knew the exact route. In fact, as I entered the old neighborhood, I saw three big fire engines roaring by—sirens wailing like sobbing mothers in mourning—and I knew—somehow—that all I had to do was follow them. We were headed in the same direction.

When I got there, the school was burning down. Dozens of fire-hoses sprayed out water and chemicals, but I could see that it was useless. The building was going to burn to the ground.

I walked up to the building, close enough that I could feel the heat of the flames on my face. I wondered if anyone was stuck inside. I looked around and saw hundreds, maybe thousands of teenagers—stunned looks on their blackened faces—watching as flames from their school building shot higher and higher. Among the young students, I saw Judah—old and pale—crying bitterly, and swaying back and forth, while reading a book. He ran over to me and tore his shirt as a sign of mourning. As I—filled with guilt—reached up to my collar to tear my own shirt, I heard the almost deafening sound of a teenager shrieking in pain. Judah and I looked toward the sound—coming from the doomed building. Staring into my friend Judah's green eyes, I saw that he recognized the voice, as I did, it was young, female, and filled with the unforgettable agony of flesh and life burning away.

Converting the Jews

For my thirteenth birthday, my parents bought me an electric chair. The kind devout Levites wear on a chain around their necks. After twenty five years, I still wear mine. I finger it now, as I sit in front of my computer console, and attempt to compose my article. The chief Levite-Rabbi of New York has asked me to respond to the claims of the Israeli Government that the Holy Joshua Levi was indeed a terrorist, and did, in fact, deserve the death penalty. With tired eyes, I read the Government statement.

"Meaning no harm, or disrespect to practitioners of other faiths (even the most bizarre of other faiths) the Republic of Israel, nonetheless feels it necessary to respond to the libelous allegation that, more than one hundred years ago, Rabbi Joshua Levi, the leader of a Messianic sect, was unjustly tried, convicted and executed for murder and terrorism. We have searched our computer records, conducted an investigation, and we are, with great reluctance, releasing our conclusion. The investigation shows, beyond a shadow of a doubt, that Levi was a terrorist, and was guilty of premeditated murder. Our report includes transcripts of several eye-witness accounts, and perhaps more importantly, tape recordings, photographs, and video taped evidence of Levi's order to murder the Israeli Prime Minister. We further find that Levi, and his followers, contributed to the Anti-Jewish terrorist campaign of the Muslim Brotherhood, a campaign which resulted in the deaths of nearly one hundred innocent victims. We must also stress that, although we no longer practice capitol punishment for any crime, Levi, under the laws of his time, deserved the punishment meted out. Again, we wish to cause no offense to the devout Levites among us, but we must respond to the dangerous libel that a responsible Israeli government executed an innocent man . . ."

I rub my eyes, and try to block out a coming headache. I have been sitting at my console for over an hour, and have not written a word. I am tired. I take a sip of wine. I crave another cigarette, but I know I have had too many. I wish Mary were here to massage the back of my neck, to pour her smooth fingers over my tight back and aching temple.

I think of the arrogance of the Israeli government. Releasing evidence after one hundred and twenty years. The eyewitness reports could easily have been made up, photographs and videotapes doctored by computers. They force us to call them liars. Yet they know it is we who will not be believed. We are a small minority—there are approximately 2 million Levites in the world of six hundred million Jews, over a billion Muslims, and another billion Hindus and others. I am appalled—distressed. My heart fills with anger. I take another sip of wine. I hate the arrogant Israelis, and their Jewish puppets in the United States. They are oppressors—subtle, mischievous, evil tyrants. They use their economic might to tear at us—to intimidate and convert us. And they are clever. Most of the overt forms of discrimination are gone. Even I, a known Levite intellectual can get an appointment at a Jewish University. They tempt us, allow us glimpses of their corrupt power structure, invite our cooperation. But they're out to destroy us, destroy all of the followers of Joshua, all of the sons and daughters of the chair. They will electrocute us as they electrocuted the Messiah, our prince of peace. Unless we stop them. And yet I am so tired.

Fading slowly but surely into unconsciousness, I reflect on the history of Jewish-Levite relations. After Joshua was electrocuted in Tel Aviv, the Zion government tried to round up all of Levi's followers. Joshua had been accused of being the mastermind behind the plot to assassinate Prime Minister Yaakov Ariel. He was executed quickly and quietly, while the Israelis attempted, in one fell swoop, to eliminate the entire Levite movement. Hundreds more were arrested, and, according to our Levite records, hundreds more were killed. But the power of Joshua was not of this earth. During this dark time of persecution most of the movement managed to escape to the United States—a Jewish country, but a more tolerant one. My grandparents were among those early refugees who carried on the work of the Messiah away from the corrupt reaches of the nationalist government in the Holy Land. We found a home in this more accepting country, but the discrimination, the ridicule, the bigotry was relentless. Officially, America has no state Religion, but with non-Messianic Jews making up ninety percent of the population, our little sect was battered and beaten. We were forbidden to preach our gospel. Evangelizing was prohibited, in the name of their corrupt, effete form of pluralism. We could not bear witness to the resurrection of Joshua, to his miracles, to his grace, to his love. To his divinity. We are commanded to preach the word of the Messiah, but American law, and certainly Israeli law, forbids proselytizing. The Jews of America let us be, but do not let us fulfill our mission.

Yet we flourish. The word has gotten out. We are one half a million souls in America, and another half a million in Israel, the corrupt Zionist stronghold. The word has spread, and we are growing.

I type a paragraph of introduction. It is garbage—no zest, no life, it is only cliched outrage. I am deathly tired. My nights with Mary have thrown me into an unrelieved exhaustion. The words from my screen blur in and out of focus, they form unintelligible lights that sparkle and illuminate the room. I take another sip of wine. My head floats and then drops. I fall asleep.

I dream of Mary. We are making love, her soft, tan body working it's way at mine filling me with awe and splendid pleasure. Her long black hair runs down my back, and creeps between my legs with a soft intensity. Her lips, delicate and soft, find the hidden parts of my body. Her breasts run over me. "Arise, my love," she whispers, "Arise and come away." She purrs with pleasure and calls out my name. We have been making love for hours, for days, for weeks, we do nothing but make love. She inside of me, I inside of her. I am hot.

My dream is interrupted. I see Joshua, sitting behind Mary, I watch him through strands of Mary's thick black hair. Joshua stares back at me, from his electric chair, his face kind but disapproving. Mary suddenly disappears. I sit up. I am naked, and alone with my Lord.

"Judah," he says softly. "Are you ready?" He is just as I have imagined him, young, frail, his beard and long hair smooth and pure, his eyes kind and strong.

"Yes, my Lord." My voice quivers. Yet I am not afraid.

"Are you my servant?" he asks.

"Yes. Oh yes."

"The flesh is corrupt, Judah. It's pleasures are never to be trusted. Do you understand me, my love?"

"I understand," I say. I am his love.

"It is the spirit that matters, my love, the body is weak and too easily tempted. Do you comprehend, Judah?"

I nod. I do.

Joshua looks at me, his arms strapped to the chair, his legs manacled. "I need you Judah. It is time. I must begin the finish of my work on earth. I choose you to assist me. Can you refuse?"

I cannot, I want to say, but I am speechless. Joshua goes on. His gentle voice fills me with indescribable pleasure.

"You do not need to respond to the insinuations of the Israeli government. Trouble yourself no more with your response. We have more important things to do than to prepare propaganda. Strengthen yourself, my love. There is work ahead." He disappears. I am alone with my computer console.

Mary comes to see me the next morning. She brings me breakfast and the morning newspaper. I have slept on my office couch, in my clothes. I am groggy, and shakily, I sit up. Mary kisses me, brushes my hair back with her hand, and hands me the paper and a cup of coffee. The coffee smells rich, but forbidding. I put it aside. "The Israeli statement made the cover of the *Chronicle*," she says, her voice alarmed, but sweet. "It's a big story, Judah." She is excited. "What are you going to write?" She smiles at me, a fresh, dimpled smile.

I get up and stretch. I look at Mary, her ringlet-shaped eyes as welcoming as I have ever seen them, and feel a tinge of desire. I look away. "There is no need to respond to those lies," I say. "There is greater work."

"But Judah," she says. "Their evidence is so damaging. I saw on the news last night a videotape of Joshua ordering a bombing. And there are photographs of him and the Muslim Brotherhood. We can't just ignore this . . ."

"It's lies," I say. "Anyone with a computer can doctor videotapes. Besides why would they wait a hundred years to release this stuff. Obviously they just decided to put it together."

"Well," Mary says, "They say they didn't want to offend the Levites—they wanted to be tolerant to the new religion. But why don't you respond—you can accuse them of deceit, of manufacturing evidence. Isn't that what Rabbi Jacob asked you to do?"

I wave her off. I answer to a higher authority than Rabbi Jacob, but it is too early to explain this to Mary. My life has changed in ways that make Rabbi Jacob irrelevant.

Mary looks at me. She is confused. I am distant—unaffectionate. I have not yet embraced her, or kissed her, but she is too polite, too devoted to say anything.

"Will I see you tonight?" she asks innocently, as if she is asking me to tea, though of course, we both know what she has in mind. Our love affair has been heated by a constant physicality ever since we met, three months ago, at a Levite social. She is the niece of a Levite-Rabbi I know well, she is a righteous daughter of Joshua. Righteous, but active. I love her. These three months have been the happiest of my life. How sad that it must end. I look at Mary, admiring her long hair, her clear face. The way of Joshua can be difficult, his love so demanding.

"Mary," I say. I pause and look at her, so loyal, so loving, so innocently erotic. How to explain? "The flesh is so weak, so corruptible."

She nods. She has no idea what I'm talking about.

I decide to come right out with it. "Joshua has appeared to me," I say. "Our Lord Joshua. In a dream. He disapproves of my fornication. He has told me to become celibate."

She stares at me, unbelieving. Nervously, she reaches for the electric chair she wears around her neck, running her fingers up and down the gold chain, in a feverish, worried gesture. She is

75

confounded. Her eyes show concern and dread. She stammers at me, "J-J-Judah, have you lost your mind? Joshua spoke to you? The Messiah Joshua? Our Lord? Do you know what you're saying?"

I look her right in the eyes. I am intensely sincere. "He has chosen me," I say. "I know it. He has called me."

"Called you for what?" she asks. She is in a panic. She loves me, but thinks me insane. She reaches out for my hand, but I pull away. She starts to cry. Our relationship, she realizes is ending. She has lost me to, of all people, her Lord, Joshua Levi.

"Called for service." I answer, stoic, unemotional. "For service," I say. "And there is no room for you. The flesh is weak, corrupting. We have been corrupted. Joshua tells us that there can be no more. He has commanded me."

"You're crazy, Judah!" she cries out. She is quite angry. "Why would he speak to you? You must have been drunk, you haven't slept enough, you're worried about your job. The rebuttal is too much for you. Snap out of it, Judah—you're human. You're not some prophet." She begins to cry. I am unmoved.

"Leave me," I say. I need take no more of this. Joshua has called me his love.

Mary tries to touch me, to rub my cheek. I cannot risk the soft, inviting touch of her hand. Rudely, I brush her away. In tears, she repeats my name. She tells me she loves me. I ignore her. Finally she drops her newspaper and leaves.

I am tired. I feel as if I have not slept at all, as if I had spent the entire night working, or exercising vigorously. I realize that I am filthy with sweat, and that I need a shave. I fall back on the couch and light a cigarette. The smoke burns my lungs, and I cough twice. I smoke too much. I have been drinking too much. I have a headache. I am feeling quite unwell. I pick up Mary's newspaper, the *San Francisco Chronicle*, and find the story about Joshua. I read as if I am in a trance.

. . . The Israeli government, for the first time has produced electronic proof that the so-called Messiah, the founder of a now worldwide religion was, in fact, a leader in a vicious Muslim terrorist group. Tapes have been released of Joshua Josephson instructing a group of terrorists on how to use the kind of plastic explosives that killed the Israeli Prime Minister, and four other Cabinet members. The tape also has Joshua giving the order to carry out the assassination. Voice analysis confirms that the voice heard on the tapes is the voice of Joshua Levi, the religious leader.

The Israeli government further provided photographic and video taped evidence showing Levi meeting and instructing members of the Muslim Brotherhood. One video tape has the religious leader pointing an Uzi (a late twentieth century automatic weapon) at members of the terrorist gang and accusing them, in harsh language, of cowardice.

Levi, and a number of his followers, began a break-off religion in the late 1980's, about one hundred and twenty years ago. Levi's followers claim that he was the Messiah, and the son of God, born to a virgin mother. Levi himself was vague about these claims, but, to his dying day, refused to deny them.

Levi preached a religion of love and forgiveness. He put himself in contrast to what he called the "onerous and hateful demands of Jewish law." Levi's followers claimed that God had revoked Jewish law (the Hallachah) and had substituted for it, belief in the divinity and saving grace of Joshua.

Joshua was executed in 1991 after being convicted of being behind the terrorist bombing which took the lives of four senior government officials in Israel, including the prime minister. The execution took place at a particularly unsteady time in Israeli history, when bombings by the Muslim Brotherhood had become common. For a period of three years, Israel reinstated the ancient death penalty for terrorist crimes. Levi was one of two people executed because of the new law. The death penalty was revoked a few years after his death.

The recent findings have thrown the Levite community into confusion. So far no official comment has come from the Levite church in San Francisco, the largest Levite community in the world. The Levites have traditionally denied the guilt of their founder and accused the Israeli government of perverting justice in a show trial. The new evidence, against a leader who called for peace and love, certainly calls into question basic tenets of the young religion . . .

The article continues in this slanderous vein. Even in America they lie, pervert, persecute, sneer, and libel. They defame the holy name of our Lord. Bleary eyed, I stare at the newspaper. My rage is like a narcotic, I feel myself sputtering involuntarily, like I am drugged. I take a drag on my cigarette, and feel the angry fatigue overwhelm my body. I fall asleep. I dream.

I dream I am in a large room in a stone house. I am sitting on a dirt floor, leaning against a stucco wall. There is a vague odor of camel dung in the air. The room is cool; the ceiling is high. In the distance, I hear the discordant sound of a muezzin—the Muslim call to prayer. I see three men in flowing white robes and khafyehs arguing with each other in Arabic. I know it is Arabic, even though it is a language I've never heard. Each of the men is holding what looks like a twentieth century automatic weapon. Suddenly a door opens, and Joshua Levi, also wearing a white robe, but without the khafyeh, bursts into the room. He is carrying a box of plastic grenades. He talks softly to the men. He speaks Arabic, but I understand what he is saying. I listen.

"My brothers," he says. "Do you know what these are?" His long beard is streaked with dust. The Muslims carefully take out the grenades—treating them with care as if they were new born babies—and examine them.

"These are our salvation," says Joshua. "With these we will finally destroy the Israeli dogs. We will have revolution."

The Muslims are silent. They look at the white grenades. They look at their automatic weapons. One of them glances at me, but quickly turns away. There is a long silence in the room. We all listen to the sound of the muezzin coming from outside the stone house, calling the faithful to prayer. I realize that I am in Jerusalem. I have traveled back in time, back to the late twentieth century.

"We agree, my brother," one of them says finally. "We will carry out the plan." All of them embrace. "God will have mercy," Joshua says.

He looks at me, his kindly eyes shining. "And you, Judah," he says. "Will you take a grenade?" He digs another white bomb out of his box and offers it to me, his hand outstretched and beseeching. The grenade looks like a flower. "Will you join us on our crusade, as glorious as any crusade ever carried out in God's history? Will you join me?"

The Muslims disappear. I am alone with my Lord, alone in the cool stone house with the smell of dung hanging in the air. I take the proffered grenade.

"Terrorism?" I whisper. My mouth is dry.

"Love," he answers.

"Murder?" I ask. "Killing?" I think of Mary.

"Salvation," he says. "Grace. Redemption. World peace. Love. Eternal, everlasting heroic Love. Only Love."

I wake up. I feel refreshed, as if I had slept soundly for the first time in weeks. I am no longer sweating, I am no longer disturbed. My headache has disappeared. I feel clean. I feel wonderful. Without bothering to wash up, or even change clothes I go into my bedroom. I pack a small knapsack with just a few items. I leave my apartment without locking the door. I'll never return. I know exactly what I have to do.

An Intermarriage

Judah, a Baal Teshuvah, that is a newly pious Jew, was returning to the United states for his sister's wedding. Actually, he was returning in order to prevent his sister's wedding. She intended to marry a non-Jew, but Judah intended to do all he could to stop her. He was in an airplane—El Al flight 003 to New York. The movie *Honey I Shrunk the Kids* was playing on the small screens dotting the aisle, but Judah was otherwise occupied. He was studying Rabbi Jacob Blau's book on how to stop intermarriages. His Rosh Yeshiva, Rabbi Feldstern had recommended it to him. He rested the large book on his airline table, and read carefully: "You must be sensitive, but firm," it said. "Stress to the Jewish partner how their action, in a passive but sure way, continues the job begun by our enemies from Pharaoh to Hitler. Point out that, in fact, more Jews are lost each year to assimilation and intermarriage than any antisemite could ever have dreamed. By denying the possibility of a next generation, a Jew who marries a non-Jew is continuing to the work of the Nazis."

Judah remembered Rabbi Feldstern's warning. "This book is a little heavy handed," he had said, his voice heavy with a questioning kind of wisdom. "All that guilt, I'm not sure it does any good. But she's your sister, you should do something. Try the thing with the Sefer Torah." The book recommended laying a Torah scroll on a table and asking the Jewish partner if he or she would be willing to spit on it. If they refused, one should explain that intermarrying is far worse than spitting on one Torah scroll; it is equivalent to desecrating every existent holy book. Judah wondered where he could get hold of a Torah scroll.

The roar of the plane engines sounded suddenly soothing to Judah. He put down his book, and looked up at the movie. He removed his thick glasses, and rubbed his hand over his face, his bushy black beard stinging the palm of his hand. He was tired, he hadn't slept in two days. He put his head up against an arm rest, and drifted off to sleep.

He dreamt that his sister and Rabbi Feldstern were dancing at a wedding, the tall Rosh Yeshiva, with the striking silver and black coat, fur hat, and long beard dwarfing Judah's petite sister. They were dancing a German waltz, the sweet music carrying them both past an admiring crowd of well wishers. Judah's sister was dressed all in white, in a long frilly dress which looked suspiciously like a wedding gown. After a while, Judah realized that, in fact, it was their wedding—his sister Dina was marrying his Rosh Yeshiva. This confused Judah since he knew that Rabbi Feldstern was already married, and had eight children. Still he could not help but feel proud that his sister had acquired such a renowned Torah scholar. Judah went up to them, and hugged them both tightly. Tears of joy rolled down his cheeks; he was as happy as he could possibly imagine. As the three of them were locked in an embrace, Judah's armrest jerked up, and he snapped awake. A stewardess was speaking over the public address system.

"Ladies and gentlemen, please do not panic. I repeat do not panic." The airplane rocked violently, spilling over coffee cups, and papers. The voice from the speaker, shrill and edgy, went on. "We are experiencing some engine trouble. Our pilots are dealing with the problem. Please remain seated and keep your seat belts securely fastened. If the oxygen masks are released, please remember to put the mask firmly over your mouth and breathe normally. "I repeat," the voice said, as the plane lurched to the right, and then to the left, forcing Judah's face into the back of the seat in front of him, "We are attempting to control the situation. Our pilots are experienced. Please do not panic." As her voice clicked off, all of the oxygen masks on the plane dropped from their compartments. Judah instinctively grabbed for his, attached the elastic around his head and began to breathe deeply. He looked out the window, as the airplane's wings twisted back and forth, and noticed the blue water of the Atlantic Ocean coming towards them. The plane was heading downward. Judah began praying.

"My God," he whispered, "Please forgive all of the sins I have committed against you, whether willingly or unwillingly. Accept me with open arms into your embrace. And please forgive and accept my death as the atonement for the sin of my mother, who is now living—outside of marriage—with a non-Jew. And forgive my father for his crime of adultery. Please bless my sister Dina, and prevent her from ruining her life with a gentile. Help her see the light of your Torah. Shma Yisrael," he said quickly, "Adonay Eloheinu Adonay Echad." He closed his eyes as the plane's downward lurch jolted his stomach.

The plane did not crash. The pilots struggled bravely and managed an emergency landing on an airstrip in New Jersey. Judah, along with everyone else on the plane, thanked God, and slid down the inflated slides on to the tarmac. Relatives of the passengers crowded around the outside of the airplane, embracing loved ones, but no one was there to meet Judah. He hadn't told anyone, not his parents, his sister, or any of his former friends, that he was flying in that day. He grabbed his backpack which he had carried with him on the plane, and found a taxi to take him to his mother's new home in Franklin Lakes.

He had never been there before. In fact he hadn't seen his mother in over a year—since he'd left for Israel. Her new home, which she'd built with her millionaire boyfriend, was a tudor style mansion, with a shining white exterior, four scupltures on the enormous, green lawn, and a long twisting driveway as big as many city blocks. Judah's taxi traveled up the driveway and stopped at the front of the house. Judah took his dirt encrusted pack out of the back seat of the car, gave the taxi driver all the money he had, straightened out his black bowler hat, buttoned his long black coat, brushing off the two day accumulation of dust, and wandered around the grounds of the mansion. It was a hot August day. Judah's heavy clothes caused streams of perspiration to trickle through his whole body, but he didn't really mind. He shielded his eyes from the sun by tilting his bowler hat, and gaped at the mansion. "Ribono shel olam," he whispered to himself—"Master of the Universe." It was an expression he had learned from Rabbi Feldstern, an expression of surprise and amazement.

He found his mother sunning herself in a chaise lounge next to the swimming pool in back of the house. She was wearing a yellow one piece bathing suit, and a white beach hat. Her eyes were closed. Judah approached her from the back of the lounge.

"Mother," he said softly. "Mother."

She didn't stir.

"Mother," he said, a little louder. Still nothing. "Eemah!" he said loudly.

She opened her eyes. "Who's there?" she said.

"It's me, Eemah." he said, standing next to her.

She stared at him, squinting through her sunglasses. "Who are you?" she said putting up her hands.

"It's me, Eemah." he said, scratching his thick beard. "Yehudah."

She looked at him, and stood up. "Judah?" she said.

"Yehudah." he answered. "It's Yehudah now."

"My God," she squealed, "My God, it is you. You've got a beard, a coat—my God, Judah, you've become a Hasid. My God, look at you." She jumped up, and tried to hug him. He held her politely.

"My plane almost crashed," he said.

She stepped back. "Oh dear," she said. "Judah, are you all right?" She reached out for his face, brushing his beard. "Oh dear."

"I prayed for you," he said. "I prayed that God should forgive you."

She took her hand away, and looked at him, stunned.

81

"Forgive me for what, Judah?" she asked, her eyes brightening with anger.

"Yehudah," he said. "My name is Yehudah. I asked God to forgive you for your sinful life. For living with a man—a non-Jew yet—without marrying him. For denying yourself and your people. For being a disgrace to God."

"Judah!"

"Yehudah!" he said loudly. "My name is Yehudah."

"Christ!" she said. "I don't care what your name is. Don't pray for me! This is a sin I'm enjoying. I don't want you to wipe out this particular sin. You know why I'm living with Thomas. He won't marry me. And I don't want to get married again anyway. I'm happy for once in my life, and you're praying for me."

"There is a law, Eemah," Judah said. "A God."

"Don't call me Eemah, Judah. I'm your mother. And don't tell me about the law. Tell your father about your precious law. You and your father are such law abiding Jews—tell him how to live his life—but don't talk to me about it. I'll live with whoever I want—I'll sleep with whoever I want. I'm way past the point of being lectured to on sexual ethics. Lecture your father—don't lecture me."

"He has also sinned," Judah said.

"Judah, my God, Judah—what's happening to you? Your father's Judaism has infected you so much that you even use it against him. That harsh Mosaic morality. I lived with it for twenty two years. And then I got screwed by it. Well screw you, screw both of you. I'm staying with Thomas." She lay back down in her lounge chair. "You can take a swim, if you'd like Judah. Thomas won't be home until this evening. Put your bag in the guest room next to the terrace. That's the room we had built for you."

He picked up his backpack. "Where is Dina?" he asked.

She took off her sunglasses and squinted at her son. "Don't bother her, Judah," she said insistently. "Don't mess around with her. She's happy. She's in love. Don't hurt her."

"She's ruining her life," Judah said. "She's destroying our family."

She put back on her sunglasses. "You're father destroyed the family," she said calmly. "Talk to him. I'm not telling you where Dina is. Tomorrow she'll be married, and out of this family. Find her yourself."

Judah took his bag and went into the kitchen, where he found his mother's purse. He took out her car keys. Dropping his pack in the guest room, he snuck outside to the large driveway, and found his mother's Buick next to two Porsches and a Cadillac. He drove toward Manhattan, to his father's synagogue.

82

Judah's father was a Rabbi at a large mid-town synagogue. Two years before, right after Judah's college graduation, he'd had an affair with a woman quite younger than he. Eventually, his wife discovered the affair, and left him. He married the younger woman, and they were planning on having children. Judah stopped speaking with him after he'd heard about the infidelity. In fact, it was very shortly after, that he'd met Rabbi Feldstern, who convinced him to come and study at his Yeshiva in Jerusalem. Rabbi Feldstern had assured him that his father's problem was the decadence of American Jewish life, and the moral emptiness of Conservative Judaism. Judah felt that he had saved himself by leaving America in the nick of time—right before he might have been forever lost to Torah-values, forever corrupted by the moral degradation of his father's life.

He double parked the car right in front of his father's synagogue and went right to the office. He breezed past the outer secretaries, and barged in. His father, a tall, attractive man in his early fifties, was sitting at his desk reading a letter. He looked up at his bearded son.

"Judah," he said calmly, after studying his face for a few moments.

"It's Yehudah."

"Yes, of course," he said. "Yehudah. How are you Yehudah?" he asked. "Please sit."

"How can you allow this wedding?" Judah demanded—his eyes burning with intensity. "How could you have let this happen? It's a disgrace—a shanda. I've come here to stop this calamity—this abomination. Where is Dina?"

The Rabbi studied his son. "I imagine she's at home right now," he said quietly. "She has an apartment on the West Side. She's trying on her wedding dress."

"I need a Sepher Torah," Judah said. "It's an emergency," he added.

"Yehudah, please sit down. It's been over a year. It's good to see you. Tell me about yourself."

"My plane nearly crashed."

"Judah!"

"My life flashed before me. All of it. I have a deeper understanding of myself—and of everyone around me. I forgive you, Abba. I've discovered the beauty of forgiveness. God forgives. And I honor you. But you must tell me where Dina's apartment is. I think I can talk her out of this tragic mistake. Please," he said. "I only have two days. I'm going back on Wednesday." Judah tried to stop his voice from rising with too much emotion. He felt his cheeks turn hot and red underneath his beard.

"Yehudah—Yehudah," his father said, his voice also shaking just a little. "Please sit down with me for a while . . . I . . . I want to hear about you."

"I can't, Abba." he said quickly. "I honor you, but I can't. Please. Dina's address," he said. "She's my sister."

His father took out a pen, and wrote down the address. Judah grabbed it, and ran out of the office, his father watching him go.

He stopped in the small chapel on the way out. It was a small, dark room of about fifty dusty seats. A modest, brown ark stood on a round table below the words, woven into a tapestry, "Know before whom you stand." Judah had been bar mitzvahed in that room—both he and his father wanting a short unostentatious ceremony. He remembered, for a moment, how happy he had been that day, and how proud his father had seemed. He wondered, again for a moment, if he would ever possess the moral elan necessary to allow his father back in his life. Rabbi Feldstern and his Yeshiva had blessed him with the certainty of faith, and with the sweet assurance of an unyielding commitment. It was that religious rigidity which had allowed him to forgive and even, without shame, to love his father. But the same unerring structure prevented him from reaching out in friendship, or even responding to his father's entreaties. He felt sad, terribly sad. But he had to see Dina. He had a job to do, and no more time to waste.

He opened the ark and took out a miniature Torah scroll, hiding it in his coat. He rushed out of the building, and drove to his sister's apartment.

As he was stuck in traffic, on that humid Manhattan day, as hot air poured in through the air vents, and sweat, in a misty stream poured off his fuzzy beard, Judah thought about Dina. He was a year older. When they had both been young children, Judah had been certain that they would one day get married. He had suspected that marrying one's sister was something out of the ordinary, but he knew that somehow they would manage. When he was four and she was three, they went through a pseudo-marriage ceremony, Judah giving Dina a ring of yellow dandelions. Dina had accepted the yellow ring with a brief kiss on Judah's smooth cheek, and the children had a secret between them which lasted for many years. They were really man and wife.

Growing up, they were constant playmates—much more comfortable with each other than with ordinary friends. They started a secret club which only they could join—and built a tree house in the woods for club meetings. They were so close, their parents became a little concerned, and urged them to find other play partners. But nothing broke the bond between them. Even when they got a little older, they were nearly inseparable. In high school, they arranged their class schedules so that they could be together for most of the day, and drive home together in the afternoon. They were best friends. After Judah was admitted to Harvard, Dina studied for hours on end, so that she could also get in. At Harvard, they lived in the same dorm, and shared the same friends.

Judah had always considered himself the stronger of the two. He helped Dina study—made sure she did her laundry—talked with her about boys—helped her through college. He, naturally, adored his sister, but he thought of her as fragile, and even a little weak. He considered it part of his obligation as the older brother to keep his sister together, to keep a watchful eye on her.

When the two of them learned of their parents' separation, and of their father's affair, Judah worried most about Dina. She seemed to take the news very badly. She refused to talk to either her father or mother, and even began avoiding Judah. She started to drink. Judah would see her in bars around Cambridge laughing hysterically, and falling over like a drunk. She began telling people that she was an orphan. She would cry, or walk out of the room at the mention of her father. She refused to attend Judah's graduation since she knew her parents would be there. Judah worried about her, but she wouldn't discuss any aspect of her parent's life. She would only see Judah if they could go out for drinks.

It was one night, a cool spring evening, after he'd had a melancholy time drinking with Dina, that he met Rabbi Feldstern. He wandered into Harvard Hillel, where the Rabbi was speaking on family purity. The talk was over, and the young, but wise looking Rabbi—nattily dressed in a dark suit and black bowler hat—was chatting with some students. He looked up as Judah walked in. Judah immediately noticed a grey kindness coming from the Rabbi's eyes, a warmth which made Judah almost want to cry. They reminded him of a kind of primal comfort which he had long since lost. Judah thought that they looked like the gentle eyes of God. They radiated, Judah thought, with everything which was true, with all certainty and beauty. He'd had a number of rum and cokes that night, and was feeling a bit woozy. But Rabbi Feldstern's eyes liberated some kind of sentimental impulse in him, and he actually felt tears welling up. The Rabbi noticed the sudden power of Judah's reaction, and excused himself from the crowd of students, walking over to speak with Judah. They talked that night for five hours, until four in the morning. Two days later, Judah left for Israel.

He'd talked to his sister only once since then, when he'd called her long distance from his Yeshiva. The connection had been poor, and neither said very much. Judah had later written her a letter trying to explain his new way of life. She hadn't written back, until—three weeks before—he'd gotten a brief card inviting him to her wedding. She was marrying Chris James,

85

someone they had both known at Harvard for two years. A nice enough guy—but a non-Jew.

Judah rang the bell of her apartment. Dina answered, her long brown hair draped across her shoulders, brushing her face. She wore a tan T-shirt, and blue jeans. She was thinner than Judah had ever remembered, but her face seemed bright and healthy. She was, Judah thought, as beautiful as he'd ever seen her, her girlish figure somehow transformed into a sculpted form of real allure. He noticed a white wedding gown hanging on a doorknob in a corner of the crowded studio apartment.

Dina stared at Judah, whose face was still covered with a dark and sticky perspiration. His beard looked like it had been dipped in muddy water. They both looked at each other, standing in the doorway, for a few moments, until Dina's startled glance turned into a glimmer of recognition.

"Judah!" she said at last.

Judah took the Torah scroll out of his coat pocket. He shoved it in his sister's face. "Can you spit on this?" he asked, his voice firm and calm. "Can you bring yourself to do that."

Dina looked at the scroll. "What is it?" she asked.

Judah walked past her into the apartment. He found the small dining room table and laid the Torah scroll out as far as it would unroll. He motioned for Dina.

"This is a Sefer Torah!" he said. "This is our holiest book; this is the book which has sustained us through two thousand years of torture and oppression. This is our life, our water, our sustenance. You know as well as I do what it is," he said. He was gesticulating wildly as he spoke, sweat pouring off his face. "Spit now on this book!" he said. "Spit on it, trample it, light it on fire, rip it to shreds. Can you?"

She walked out of the room, into the bathroom, closing the door. Judah heard water running into a sink. He followed her into the bathroom. She was crying, trying to wash her face as tears continued to stream down her cheeks. They looked at each other.

"Judah," she said tearfully, wiping her eyes, her voice sounding lonely and exhausted. "Judah, Judah. It's good to see you." She stopped crying.

"It's good to see you, Dina. Please don't marry this guy."

She started crying again, covering her eyes with her small hands, and shaking her head.

"Judah," she said through the tears. "You know how everything's changed. You've changed more than anyone. I have to go on with my life." she said. "I love him."

Judah felt his self-confidence drain, as his sister continued weeping in front of him. He hadn't expected her to fall apart, and her tears somehow robbed him of his righteous anger. He wanted to talk to her about Hitler, about Pharaoh, about the disintegration of the Jewish people. But he lost all of his urgency, as he looked at his sister.

"Dina," he said softly, almost whispering. "The family—the shame. How," he said, shaking his head. "How can we go on. What's left?"

Dina blew her nose and looked at her brother. "We're still family, Judah." she said. "We've just made different choices. We've got different lives now. We all have our own ideal. We're all doing what we want. You more than anyone, Judah—you've made your choice, and we all have to accept that. I'll try to accept that now, to be more tolerant. We all need to be more tolerant. I have to marry Chris, tomorrow because it's what I need to do—I need him in my life." She touched his arm. "Judah, don't block us out again. Stay for awhile. Come to the wedding Judah, even Dad said he would sneak in."

Judah shook his head. "I don't know," he said. "I don't know."

He stayed with her for another hour. They spoke politely—sometimes intimately—about the past year. Then he took the Sefer Torah and returned to his mother's house in Franklin Lakes.

The next day was the wedding. Judah was scheduled to fly back to Israel that evening. He told his mother that he wasn't going to the wedding. She left without arguing, but first wrote him a check for five thousand dollars. She also left him a thousand dollars in cash. Judah called a taxi to take him to the airport.

On the way, Judah asked the driver to take him to the Plaza Hotel in midtown where Dina was getting married. He told him to wait, with the meter running, while Judah peeked into the wedding.

He found the hall as the procession was ending. Dina, dressed in a flowing white gown, was walking down a red-carpeted aisle with her soon to be husband. A judge stood at the edge of a wide pulpit, and was about to begin the ceremony. Judah found a seat in the rear of the auditorium, and settled in unnoticed.

As the judge began to speak, Judah noticed that Dina was staring at him. Her lips were moving, and it seemed very much like she was trying to say something to Judah. He stared back at her, puzzled, and listened to the judge drone on. Dina continued to move her lips, and stare at her brother. Judah thought of interrupting the ceremony, of rushing down the aisle and sweeping Dina away. A dramatic scene developed in his brain, a scene of redemption. He would come to the rescue, tear Dina away at the last possible moment. But he was caught, immobile, and all he could do was watch as his sister seemed to call out to him. He grabbed the sides of his chair, but could not bring himself to get up. He stared at Dina as the judge finished asking her if she took Chris to be her husband. "I do." she said, and Judah saw that she was no longer looking at him. In fact, now he wasn't sure that he hadn't imagined the whole thing. All he saw now was the strange portrait of his now happy sister locked in an embrace with a new husband. He watched for a few moments as the well wishers gathered around the new couple. Then he ducked out of the hall, found his taxi and continued on to the airport.

Back on the airplane, Judah relaxed in his seat, tightening his safety belt. He tipped his bowler over his eyes, hoping to fall asleep. As the airplane's engines revved up, and the plane began to taxi down the runway, Judah, recalling his previous experience, felt a little nervous. He remembered that most airline crashes occur either at liftoff, or at landing. He looked around suspiciously, and decided to recite Tefillat Haderech—The Prayer for a Journey. He took a card with a printed text of the prayer out of his wallet, and mumbled the words to himself, as the airplane rose smoothly into the sky. He closed his eyes and thought of Dina.

Suddenly he started to cry—hot tears streaming down his bearded face, stinging him with a melancholy so bitter that Judah was not sure that he could stand it. He hid his face in his hands, and shook with sobbing. He continued crying—his hands trembling—as he thought of Dina. "Merciful God," he whispered to himself, and thought of Dina. "Merciful God help me. God have mercy on my soul," he said. "God have mercy." He continued crying, and continued thinking of Dina.

The Illness

1.) The Diagnosis

Judah L.'s body must have failed him in some way, since he woke up one fine morning feeling dreadfully ill. At first he thought he could ride it out without any unnecessary bother. He would lighten up on his work schedule (though his work was both difficult and important), drink orange juice and tea, take massive doses of Vitamin C, and try to get to sleep earlier. This went on for several weeks without any noticeable improvement. Finally he went to the doctor, who—finding nothing unusual in the physical examination—ordered extensive blood tests. L. received the diagnosis while sitting in his new office—a one-windowed square room that was slightly larger than his old working space. He'd gotten the use of this bigger office—which offered a fine desk with two extra drawers—when his immediate superior had been fired. He was reclining in his chair (his old chair hadn't reclined at all), staring at the ceiling when two nurses walked in.

L. thought it odd that these nurses would leave the comforts of his Doctor's spacious medical building—in uniform yet—just to pay a visit to a single patient. L. noted that their faces seemed grim. This was upsetting, he remembered that they were both normally quite cheerful.

"I'm sorry Mr. L." one of them said. She was the taller one, the attractive one. L. remembering being quite taken with her the first time she drew blood out of his veins. She had smiled sweetly as the needle pierced his skin, and the brightness of her young face had almost obscured the sharp pain of the needle. The second nurse, who at that moment looked almost on the verge of tears, was shorter, plumper. L. had some affection for her also—she seemed extraordinarily kind—still, that simple affection was nothing like the almost physical, though also somewhat melancholy, affinity he felt for the tall one.

"I'm sorry," she repeated. "We know we shouldn't be disturbing you here at your place of business. You seem so busy in this handsome office. But—well the fact is Mr. L. . . ." She cleared her throat, and then rubbed her eyes with her handkerchief. "I'm sorry sir, it's just that, well, this is just hard to say. We have some distressing news."

"The blood tests." L. said immediately, as he felt the color drain from his cheeks.

Both nurses nodded together.

L. swallowed. "The doctor has a diagnosis?" he said.

They looked at each other, the tall one facing down, the short one looking up. Their cheeks were suddenly red.

"Not exactly," said the plump one.

"Not really," said the attractive one.

"No?" said L. "No diagnosis? Then what?"

"A prognosis," they both said together. Then the one L. thought he could love said, "And I'm afraid it's not a very good prognosis."

L. felt frightened, close to panic. He was about to embarrass himself completely by running out of the office, and possibly screaming at the top of his lungs, when he suddenly found himself confused.

"But wait," he said. "How can there be a prognosis without a diagnosis?"

The nurses manipulated their necks once again, in order to stare at each other.

"Well, you see, it's very complicated," said the short one.

"It's quite involved," said the other. "It's not entirely comprehensible."

L. looked at them.

"The medical technology," said one. "Well, you see it's quite advanced."

"Yes" said the other, nodding. "And the training necessary to explain, we'll it's just . . ."

"Enough!" yelled L.

At the sound of his angry shout, L.'s tall nurse began to whimper. She took her handkerchief out of her white uniform and loudly blew her nose. "I'm sorry," she said, still crying softly, but gaining control of herself. "I didn't mean to fall apart. It's just that we've come all this way, making a private visit. You know that's very unusual. But we wanted to tell you ourselves, rather than send it to you in the mail because—well because we care so very much for you. You've touched our hearts so fully. So here we are, far from our comfortable office. And you yell at us. It's just so distressing," she said and once more began to whimper. Soon the other nurse joined her, and they were both dabbing their eyes with their clean white handkerchiefs.

L. was dumfounded. Yet, at the same time, he felt a great wave of sympathy and affection for both nurses. They had come all this way and they did care for him. He went up to them and put his arms around both of them.

"Now, now," he said. "I'm sorry I lost my temper. It's not a common thing for me to do. I apologize. It's just that I'm . . . well . . . perhaps I should speak to the Doctor."

They immediately separated themselves from L.'s embrace. "The Doctor?!" one said, sounding alarmed. "Why," said the other, equally taken aback "would you want to see the Doctor?"

"To discuss my case. My diagnosis."

The nurses looked at each other, perplexed.

"See the Doctor?" the tall one asked.

"Of course," said L.

"The Doctor, you know, is a busy man." said the plump one.

"He has quite a full schedule," offered the other. "We don't like to waste his time."

The other nodded.

L. cleared his throat. He tightened his wide gray tie—in fact it was his favorite tie—and brushed his thinning brown hair back with his hand. "I'm aware," he said. "of how busy the Doctor is. Yet I imagine that you have some influence with him. And seeing that you have some affection for me . . ." He lay his hand—lightly—on the shoulder on each nurse. ". . . as I am certainly fond of you, perhaps you can get me an appointment. I hate to impose. It's just that the prognosis . . ." he looked into the eyes of the one he liked best. "You understand," he said.

She bit her lip, but continued to meet L.'s gaze, looking deeply into his eyes.

"I'll get you an appointment," said the tall attractive one. The plump one pushed her hands into the pockets of her white uniform.

2.) The Doctor

L. was really quite fortunate. Not only did he get in to see the Doctor the very next day, he was also whisked into the office as soon as he arrived. On previous visits, L. had waited up to half an hour before being allowed into the Doctor's private chamber; that day there was no wait at all. He felt himself to be especially lucky; it was clear that his friendship with the tall skinny nurse would pay off well.

The Doctor, who had been studying some lab reports, looked up from behind his wide desk. He appeared stunned to see L., so much so that he dropped a pen on the floor, and nearly spilled his glass of water.

"Why Mr. L.," he said, after recovering the pen. "I'm really quite surprised to see you. My impression was that my nurses had given you my report." He fingered his wide, bow-tie mustache and gave a half smile.

"Well," said L. "I would not exactly call it a report. I think using the word 'report' would be rather generous. The fact is, Doctor," he said firmly—leaning forward—attempting, despite a rapidly failing will, to be assertive. "They gave me no details at all."

The Doctor sighed. He rubbed his eyes, which L. noticed were red from fatigue. He rested his forehead on his hand, allowing L. to see the Doctor's prominent and gleaming bald spot. "Details," he said softly, in a voice which demonstrated utter resignation. He looked up. "I'm sorry Mr. L. If you only knew. If you could only understand." He shook his head. "Details," he said again, this time in a whispered, introspective voice, as if he were talking to himself, as if L. were not in the room at all. Suddenly, the Doctor threw his entire face into his hands and started to cry.

L. was astounded. Here he was desperately sick, getting no better, his future darkly uncertain, and his Doctor sat at his desk—a rather nice desk at that, long and built from what looked like real Oak—and wept. L. found himself feeling helpless and quite annoyed. Yet he couldn't help himself from feeling oddly sorry for the man.

"Uh, well, Doctor," he said, fumbling for words. This attempt at communication only made the Doctor's cry louder. L. could see tears leaking through the fingers of his Doctor's thick white hands.

"You don't understand," said the Doctor, still weeping. "The Medical Journals, the rush of new information, strange new diseases that no one can figure out, each one deadlier than the next. Conventions, colleagues shouting at each other—competing, writing articles, applying for grants, new research. You can't possibly understand, my poor sweet young man, you can't possibly . . ." He looked up at L., but couldn't finish the sentence. He buried his face in his hands once again, and resumed his uncontrolled weeping. He seemed to be mumbling something through the tears. L. thought it sounded like "helpless." This went on for several minutes. The sobbing was only interrupted once when the Doctor looked up and asked L. if he was getting enough fluids. But before L. could even answer, the Doctor had laid his head down and resumed his crying.

"Well," said L. getting up from his chair. "Perhaps I should see another Doctor."

The Doctor sat up immediately, his face suddenly dry. "You don't trust my diagnosis?"

"No, no" answered L., slowly backing out of the office. "I have absolute trust in you. And in your nurses, I might add. I merely thought—a second opinion. In a case so serious . . . It seemed wise . . . perhaps a specialist . . . ?"

"A specialist?" asked the Doctor in a confused but angry voice, as if he didn't know the meaning of the word, as if L. had introduced a strange foreign language into their conversation.

"Yes it just seems . . ."

"Please leave my office, Mr. L." said the Doctor. "This is

just too distressing. You have my diagnosis. You can plainly see that there is nothing I can do. I have too much stress right now in my life to deal with a completely hopeless case. I can't be wasting my time tilting at windmills. Please leave."

In a frightened daze, L. did back out of the office. On his way out, he bumped into the tall nurse, who held him for a moment before letting go. He turned around and they looked each other in the eye. Before he could speak, his nurse shoved a thick manila folder into his hand, along with a business card.

"Take this," she said. "This is your file. All the information a specialist will need."

L. held the thick binder. It seemed awfully heavy, considering he'd only been in the office three times altogether. He was about to look through the file, when the nurse leaned down and whispered to him. Her warm breath pouring into his ear felt oddly therapeutic.

"And go see this specialist," the nurse whispered. She pointed to the business card. "But for God's sake don't tell the Doctor I gave you any of these things. His feelings are so fragile, and he means so . . . well, just don't tell him. But go see this specialist. She's brilliant. She's wonderful. I've managed to get you an appointment this afternoon. You have to go." she insisted. "Now."

L. was disappointed. He was hoping they could sit and chat, perhaps have lunch. "But," L. said aloud. "I really . . ."

"Shhh!" whispered the nurse, and looked around to see if they were being watched. "Just go," she whispered. She bent down slightly to look him in the eye. "You really don't have a choice, you know."

He nodded.

3.) The Specialist

As L. sat in the waiting room, waiting to see the specialist, it occurred to him—for an instant—that perhaps he felt better. He stood up and stretched, breathed deeply, exerted himself by bouncing up and down a few times on the balls of his feet, all the while checking to see if his symptoms returned. For a very brief moment—as he realized that he was experiencing no symptoms whatsoever—he felt a moment of unease. He was afraid that this prominent specialist would renounce L. as a hopeless hypochondriac. She would embarrass him, accuse him of indolence, call him a charlatan who was only wasting the time of those dedicated health professionals who had worked so long and hard on L.'s behalf. When L.'s symptom—after what was really no more than a second—did return, L. felt a melancholy pang of fear and helplessness which—he had to admit—was mixed with relief.

L. saw two young men waiting with him in the outer office. Both appeared thin and drawn—pale with sunken, hollow eyes. He also noticed ugly brown splotches on the arms of both the men. L. guessed that they were suffering from the same illness. One of them, he noticed, was wheezing loudly, while the other one also seemed to be having difficulty catching his breath. A lung disease, thought L. Was this new doctor, then, a lung specialist? But that would not fit his case at all. He decided to ask one of the men.

"Excuse me," he said to one of them, the one L. thought looked the most friendly, though—to be honest—both men looked dreadful. "Are you perhaps suffering from a condition of the lungs?"

The man slowly turned toward him. His chalky white face made L. think of ghosts. His wide eyes studied L.'s body. He opened his mouth slightly, but didn't say a word.

Perhaps I didn't speak loudly enough, thought L. He did have a tendency toward shyness and this unfortunate character trait often stopped him from speaking up when he should. Maybe the unfortunate wretch just hadn't heard him. He repeated the question in a loud, clear voice. This time the patient just turned away.

A nurse suddenly appeared and scolded L. "Here now," she said, wagging her finger. "Why are you pestering these men?"

"Excuse me," L. said, annoyed. "I was certainly not pestering anyone. I merely wanted to know the name of the illness these two gentleman have."

"And why is that your business?" demanded the nurse. L. felt fatigued. He longed for the company and comfort of his tall friend—kind and gentle—not at all like this angry drill sergeant of a nurse.

"I thought . . ." L. began to explain.

"You have no business harassing these men. You'll find out soon enough what illness the sick bastards have. And if you don't find out, then it was none of your affair in the first place. Now let's have some quiet. The Doctor is very sensitive to noise and she has a lot of important work to do."

Chastened, L. became quiet. He looked through the magazines on the table in front of him, but could not find anything he wanted to read. Eventually, he was called in to see the specialist.

Well, Mr. L." she said, as soon as he walked in. "This is not at all what it seems." L. was not quite sure how she, in fact, knew that he had entered the spacious office, since she hadn't even looked up and L. made very little noise when he walked. She was looking down, studying a file.

L. sat down, on a blue, naugahyde chair across from the

specialist's desk.

"This is extraordinary," said the specialist, still not looking at L., still pouring over what L. presumed were his records. "One might even say outlandish!"

"Oh?" L. said. It was all he could think of to say.

"That doctor of yours is certainly an incompetent of the first order. It's hard to see how anyone could have done a better job mucking up your case. I've always thought it was a shame that your friend the nurse would work for such an utter boob. Still, I suppose it's a living." She looked up at L. for an instant, seeming to check for a reaction. When L. just stared straight ahead—shocked, not sure how to react—she shrugged and looked back down at her papers. They sat together in silence for several minutes.

"Then," ventured L., somewhat hopefully. "The diagnosis is wrong?"

"Now, wait!" she snapped. "Just you wait. We don't need patients running around making medical judgments. There's been enough amateurism in this case. Don't you start prattling on about a diagnosis. What I can tell you is that your doctor wouldn't know a flu bug if it buzzed around his ears for hours. He wouldn't know a vaccine from vaseline. He hasn't the slightest notion of what to do with your case."

"So," said L. "Then . . . the prognosis?"

But she didn't seem to hear. She was nodding her head, and clucking in amazement at the stupidity of L.'s doctor. Suddenly she stopped and looked L. right in the eye.

"We'll need more tests," she said. "X-rays. C-T scans. Sonograms. This needs to be done right away. Immediately. Today, if possible. Do you understand me?"

"But if you could perhaps . . ."

"Mr. L. I'm afraid I'm not making myself clear. The only reason I'm seeing you at all is because I have a special fondness for your fiance, the nurse . . ."

"She's not my . . ."

"Never mind! This case has already taken up too much of my time. It's inordinately complicated, tremendously time consuming, and it's already been almost irretrievably botched by some worthless quack. You must simply do what I say." She scribbled a note on a piece of paper. "Go to this laboratory. Get this work done. X-rays, C-T scans. This is our next step, Mr. L." She looked deeply into L.'s eyes. "I mean . . ." she said, looking down again, as if she felt embarrassed, her voice suddenly softening into what might almost be called compassion, "it is *your* next step."

4.) The X-Rays

L. was strapped into a cot directly below the C-T scan. He lay prone, his arms spread out from his torso, his legs pushed tightly together. He felt a chill; the metal from the machine felt cold against his bare skin. He was entirely alone, the X-ray chamber held only him, his cot and the machine.

Lying motionless, breathing slowly, an image formed in his mind. It was his tall nurse, still in her white outfit, dancing in a ballet. Her movements were quite graceful, considering her rather awkward height, and overall gawky build. L. thought she looked like an angel. He began to think that perhaps she really was an angel. She hovered, in his vision, above him against a starry black background. Her movements were slow and beckoning. Suddenly L. heard a loud voice—deep and low, like the voice of God.

"Please breath in, and hold your breath!" it said.

L. did as he was told.

A light flashed followed by a soothing, almost melodic hum.

After a few minutes, L. heard the voice again.

"Please breath in again, and hold it!"

L., as if the voice was a presence in a burning bush, as if he were Moses asked to liberate his people, did as he was told.

5.) The Visitors

The tall nurse paid a visit to L. one evening. He was lying in his sickbed, his wrinkled white sheets pushed off, a glass of water and bottles of pills prominent on his nightstand. The nurse carried a small package tucked under her arm.

"I've brought you something that I know will help you," she said, with great enthusiasm.

L. looked at her. He had his doubts. He had tried many remedies in the course of his illness, yet he felt no better than when he'd come down with the sickness some months before. The fact is, despite everything he'd tried, he felt worse. Still he was anxious not to depress his friend and nurse. He gave her a half smile and asked her what she'd brought.

She slowly unwrapped the package—it had been wrapped in plain brown paper—and showed the contents to L. It was a videotape.

"The Marx Brothers," said the nurse. "*A Night in Casablanca*. This will cheer you up!" she said insistently. "It's good for you!"

L. sighed. He was not at all in the mood to watch a movie. It hurt his neck to lift his head up toward the TV. Also, it was getting late, L. was tired, and he really just wanted to go to sleep.

"I'm not sure . . ."

"Oh, come on!" said the nurse. "This will help you! You're altogether too gloomy sometimes. You've become a sourpuss. You need some laughs. I'll go get the machine; we can watch it in here."

"I don't think . . ."

"Judah!" she said, imploring.

He shook his head. They were quiet. "I just don't want to," L. said, finally.

The nurse grabbed the video and slammed it onto the nightstand, creating a loud thump. "You're not trying, Judah," she said angrily. "You're just not trying!"

"Excuse me?"

"You're not trying hard enough. You're being a victim. You're not taking control of yourself, you're not using your will. I'm not sure you even want to get well, you just lie here all day!"

L. was surprised. He spent his days lying down because he was ill. He didn't feel he could do much else. What else should he be doing?

"I believe I've seen just about every doctor in the city." L. pointed out. "I've gone through ever possible test. What can you be saying? I'm not trying? What can you possibly mean by that?"

"I'm not talking about seeing doctors. That's not it at all Judah. It's your energy, your . . ."

She broke off in mid-sentence and looked towards the room's entrance. L. looked also, and noticed two co-workers coming in to see him.

"We've come to visit," said one.

"Noticed you'd been out," said the other, brightly. "Asked the boss. Told us you were a bit under the weather. Thought we could cheer you up a bit." He put a small vase filled with roses on L.'s nightstand, placing it next to the Marx Brothers video tape. Then he put out his hand. It took L. a few moments to realize that his guest was actually offering to shake hands. L. reached up and gave the firmest handshake he could manage, which of course was still very weak.

L. was genuinely moved. He really hadn't known these two all that well. In fact, L. remembered an argument he'd had with one of them over whether or not to purchase a new office computer. L. had been against, the guest had been in favor, and the discussion actually became quite intense, almost bitter. Still, the fellow had clearly gotten over that argument and was making amends by visiting, even bringing along a friend with whom L. was even less acquainted. The gesture touched L., but he was still tired, and really wanted to get to sleep.

"I'm grateful, gentlemen," he said, firmly. "Really grateful.

Your thoughtfulness it's just . . . well it's overwhelming. Still I wonder if we could get together another time. Tomorrow morning, perhaps, or the next day. I'm just so tired right now and strained. I think sleep might be what I really need right now."

"Of course," said the first one.

"Quite understand," said the other. And they turned towards the door. Suddenly, however, one of them—the one L. knew better—turned around.

"Now this is your negative attitude," he said, with a clear disapproving tone. "Once again. Just like with the computer. I must say that I'm not at all surprised that you haven't gotten better. To get better one must think better. One must enjoy visitors. Watch funny movies. Think of oneself as well and whole. You'll never get anywhere with your constant, lazy negativity." He looked at his companion, who nodded in agreement. L. noticed that his nurse was also nodding.

"That's what I've been trying to tell him," she said in her most scolding tone.

"Well, you can tell him and tell him," said the visitor. "But this is a man without imagination, without daring. Wouldn't spend the money on a new computer, even though any fool could see that it's these new technologies which will be the preservation of our business. But this L.—a perfectly fine fellow, by the way, and I certainly wish him a full recovery—well, he has no openness about him. He's cheap in money, which makes him cheap in soul. You know," he said leaning close to the nurse and speaking softly, though L. heard every word. "No one in the office is at all surprised that he's taken ill."

The nurse again nodded her head, both in agreement and in disgust. The three of them—his visitors—looked at him, and L. could almost palpably feel the disapproval which emanated like a poison gas from their faces. Finally he spoke up.

"You're blaming me," L. said bitterly. "You're saying it's my fault. That I had a choice. That I can choose to get better. Can you really be saying that? That I've chosen all of this suffering? That I've determined that my life should be wretched?" L. felt like crying. Instead he reached over to his glass and took a sip of water. He also took a tissue and, while pretending to blow his nose, wiped away his few newly formed tears. When he looked up again at his friends, he noticed that they looked quite dismayed.

"We're not saying that at all," said one of his co-workers.

"Why that's absurd," said the other.

"Well it certainly seems that way," said L., hotly. "But it doesn't matter. I know that it's not my fault. I couldn't have brought on any of this, even if I'd wanted to. Like you said, I don't have any imagination. I have a cheap psyche. I couldn't have dreamed up this type of suffering." L. lay back on his pillow and stared straight up at the ceiling. He decided that he wouldn't say another word. He would wait until they all left him alone.

After a few minutes, the nurse took his hand. It felt cool. She stroked L.'s cheek and said, "My darling, we know that it's not your fault. We know that. You didn't cause your disease. I would never say that." She kept her hand up against his hot face.

"Thank you," said L. softly, trying to hold back his tears. He looked at her gratefully.

"It's just that you're not trying hard enough to get better," she said.

6.) The Rabbi

L. found the Rabbi in the far, dark corner of the Sanctuary, below the dull-crimson stained glass window. He was folding up a card table, an operation which was rendered difficult to the point of futility by the several books the Rabbi had tucked under his arm. He was about to drop all of the books, when L. rushed to him and relieved him of most of the burden. Together, without saying a word, they took the volumes—which L. could now plainly see were prayer books—and replaced them in the metal slots connected to the wooden pews. The Rabbi, L. noticed, seemed quite young and fairly vigorous. L. could not really see his face; the room was dark for one thing, and their work forced the Rabbi to keep his back turned towards L.

It was, in fact, with his back turned, that the Rabbi began to speak.

"I've heard from your Doctor, you know," he said somberly, as he walked towards the next aisle and began replacing another row of books.

L. was surprised to hear that. He didn't even know the Rabbi. He was not a member of the congregation, nor had he had much of anything to do with organized Judaism since his Bar-Mitzvah, some twenty years before. L. couldn't imagine what business his Doctor (and which doctor did he mean, anyway?) would have with this young Rabbi. The only reason he was even visiting this gloomy synagogue was because of the unpleasant encounter with his nurse, and colleagues from work. L. had the vague idea that talking with a Rabbi could make him more "spiritual." (whatever that meant), and therefore hasten his chances for recovery. He was willing to try anything. Still, L. stayed silent and went on putting away the prayer books.

"Things don't appear to be altogether hopeless," the Rabbi went on. L. noted that there was a bit of melodic tone to the Rabbi's voice—a sing-song quality that L. actually found quite appealing. "But, on the other hand," he continued. "They don't look all that good either." He shrugged, and finally turned toward L. L. saw a handsome, bearded face with thick-lensed glasses obscuring—nearly hiding—the Rabbi's light blue eyes. The Rabbi sat down on one of the hard wooden pews, and motioned for L. to do the same. He asked L. why he had come to see him.

L. was about to respond—brightly, but sincerely—that his illness had pushed him into searching for a spiritual life. But in the middle of formulating his answer, he burst out with something else entirely.

"Why am I suffering so much?" he said, and it was a demand, a furious insistence, as if he were a powerful king commanding his losing general to explain the fiasco on the battlefield. "I've been a decent man all my life," L. went on. "I'm honest. I'm not cruel. I contribute to charities. I've never been violent. I've been kind and responsible in all of my important relationships. Why am I sick? Why am I dying? Other people I know—rotten, lying bastards—I see them on the streets—manipulative cruel folks, only out for themselves. They're healthy, not a care in the world. There's a man I used to know, a lawyer I met once or twice socially. Last year he embezzled five million dollars from his business. And he got away with it. He's living on the Cayman Islands. Enjoying his dishonest life. Why do I have to go through this hell, while these others—these corrupt souls—these criminals get off scott free? Why is this happening to me?"

The Rabbi waited a few minutes before responding. He straightened out one of the prayer books. Finally, he looked at L. "Why shouldn't it happen to you?" he asked.

L. was stunned to hear that question. "Because it's unfair!" he answered.

"And you think life should be fair?"

L. thought for a moment. "I do," he said.

"Well, then," said the Rabbi. "Let me tell you a story. There was a King who had many subjects who loved him. Unfortunately, the Kingdom was surrounded by enemies. Every year there were cruel wars where many, many people suffered and died. The King was touched that his people were willing to fight and sometimes even die in order to keep the Kingdom alive. But he was upset that his people had to suffer. So he came up with an arrangement. His citizens would live in the Kingdom for a short time, and fight in the wars, and suffer along with the rest. Then, after a few years of fighting, the King would find each of his subjects a place in another Kingdom—a peaceful Kingdom, where they could live out their lives free from harm."

"Another Kingdom," L. said, softly, without sounding entirely convinced.

"If you don't like that story," said the Rabbi. "I'll tell you

100

another. There once was a righteous man who suffered for no reason. He lost his children, his wealth and finally his health. His wife told him to curse God and die. Instead he demanded an answer from God. Why was he in such pain, he called out; he didn't deserve it. Finally God answered him. He told him that he was too busy to worry about this man's problems, and anyhow the universe was a much more complicated place than this man's puny mind could ever imagine. He didn't explain why this man suffered, he just showed him there were things that people will never understand. Then he restored the man's health, and his riches."

"Job?" said L.

The Rabbi nodded. "And if you don't like that story, I'll tell you another. There once was a King that needed to provide his subjects with enough food to eat. So he invented a machine that would sweep across the fields, planting, fertilizing, watering, and finally harvesting. He set the machine to function all year round, so the people would never go without food. Unfortunately, this was a large machine, with many parts. As it made its way through the fields of the Kingdom, occasionally a child or even an adult would accidentally get in it's way. This caused great suffering and even death to those few people caught in the machine's path. And this hurt greatly disturbed the King. But he knew he couldn't stop the machine, for it was that machine which guaranteed life for the whole Kingdom."

"A machine," L. said.

"I can tell you another," said the Rabbi. "A more recent story. Once there was a King who loved his subjects with great love. This was a beautiful Kingdom, but it was surrounded by a gigantic toxic dump. It was impossible to leave the Kingdom, since entering the dump meant instant death. Unfortunately, the toxic dump did have an effect even inside the beautiful Kingdom. It occasionally generated a dreadful illness which lead to great suffering among the few that caught the disease. The people begged the King to do something about the toxic dump. He gathered his wise men, all the great thinkers of the Kingdom, but they couldn't come up with a way to either remove the dump, or cure the sickness. Yet the people continued to implore the King who—try as he might, and as well intentioned as he was—didn't have an answer. The only thing he could think of was to visit the home of any subject who caught the disease. The King would then stay with the sufferer, walk with him, sleep in the same room, talk to him, even cook meals and bring water. For if the King couldn't solve his subject's problem, at least he could demonstrate his love. And they might be slightly comforted by being in the presence of the King."

The Rabbi finished. He turned towards the pulpit and looked

at the Ark. L. looked too, and noticed a small yellow lamp hanging over the altar.

"What do you think of my stories?" the Rabbi asked.

"I quite liked them," answered L., and in fact he did think that each of the stories was helpful in it's own way. L. felt a particular compassion for all of the Kings in the story—these powerful, loving beings who suffered with their subjects. Yet, even as he considered the obvious meaning behind all of the stories, L. felt a wave of fatigue run over him. Then, thinking about the poor King in the final story—his pathos, his futile energy—L. felt his symptoms overwhelm him and he was forced to lie down, and try to rest.

7.) The End

One dark morning L. woke up, struggled out of bed, and went into the kitchen to make himself a glass of herbal tea. He'd had a rough night, his symptoms bedeviled him to the point where he'd only slept for an hour or two at the most. He would have preferred to stay in bed, but his nurse was due soon, and he wanted to look as presentable as possible.

As he sat down at the kitchen table, he realized that he'd never really felt this sickly. His symptoms announced themselves in pulsating waves all through his body. He considered calling an ambulance, but instead went to the stove and put water on to boil. With trembling hands, he set a tea bag into a glass, and poured in the boiling water. For a moment, he imagined that he was feeling a little better. Actually—he realized after a few seconds—he had stopped breathing.

He sat down on the floor, his bony rear-end bouncing against the linoleum. As if in response, he felt his heart stop beating. He tried to get up for a moment, if only to grab the tea, but it was simply impossible. All he managed was another slight bounce against the cold floor. Then he lay down and began to die.

Out of the corner of his eye, he saw a human-like figure float towards him, dressed in white. An angel, he thought, maybe the Angel of Death—coming to take me to the King. A small but rapturous smile appeared on his face as he imagined himself encompassed by love and grace. The smile disappeared, though, right before he died, leaving the world forever, as the thought occurred to him that the strange ghostly figure coming to take him—a tall, pale figure with beautiful sad eyes—may not be an angel at all, but something else—a familiar being, mortal and human.

About the Author

Philip Graubart is the spiritual leader of Congregation B'nai Israel in Northampton, Massachusetts. He has published fiction and non-fiction in many periodicals, including *Response*, *Midstream*, *Tomorrow*, *Beggar's Banquet*, and *Tikkun*. He lives in Northampton with his wife and two sons. This is his first book.